The Shadowed Moon

by

Elli Morgan

Cover Art by *Debbie Taylor*

The Wild Rose Press, Inc.
PO Box 708
Adams Basin, NY 14410-0708
Visit us at www.thewildrosepress.com

Publishing History
First Edition, 2024
Trade Paperback ISBN 978-1-5092-5593-1
Digital ISBN 978-1-5092-5594-8

Published in the United States of America

Dedication

To my Mum, the strongest person I know.
Also, to the encounters that shape us, the struggles we overcome, and the courage to conquer our inner demons.

Acknowledgements

As I write these acknowledgements, I'm a little swamped with everything that's happening in my life right now. So, the first one I want to thank is my boyfriend Fabian, without whom I'd be drowning in tasks.

The Shadowed Moon was quite a challenge for me because I couldn't relate to my main characters in the first version of the book. It took me a while to shape them the way they were supposed to be, and my manuscript often frustrated me. During that time, my friends Ann Christin and Iris encouraged me to keep writing. Thank you so much for that—this book wouldn't exist without you!

I'm also very grateful to my beta readers Audriauna, Lauren, David, Tayler, Heather, and Marissa.

Lastly, I'd like to thank my editor Lill for giving my book a chance to shine.

Part I

SURRENDER

*You say I'm a beast—
I agree. But what do you
call those who made me?*

Chapter 1

Giving in to the urge to feed, turning into the beast her kind expected her to be, and betraying the little girl she once was would be so much easier.

A light breeze carried the hunter's heady scent to Sarah as she leaned against a majestic walnut tree on this moonless night. She clenched her fists as a shudder ran through her, and every cell inside her body ached for his sweet blood.

After years of suffering at the hands of monsters, she'd mastered the art of renouncing her cravings. Pressing her body against the tree, she concentrated on the coarse bark rubbing against her skin. She could not suppress the abominable hunger forever, but her determination combined with the sensory distraction granted her control of her urges for a little while longer. Would it last long enough to talk to him and set her plan in motion?

The hunter—a young, muscular man with short, chestnut-brown hair and light stubble on his chiseled face—browsed through his phone, painfully unaware of the vampire watching him. And not for the first time. She'd followed him and his team for five days, studying their tactics and abilities from the shadows. They showed promise, although their approach of posing as bait often

1

put them at risk. With a little help from her, they'd rid the world of even more monsters.

She could have picked any group of hunters, but something about the leader of this team enthralled her. His dark eyes held the same sadness and longing she often glimpsed in the mirror. If only she could talk to him about her intentions, but hunters never listened.

She inhaled deeply. Would he pass her test and prove they were more than easy prey?

Her ankle boots echoed on the pavement of the quiet, suburban neighborhood as she approached him from behind. The *clacking* reminded her of her mother, strutting through the world like she owned it…as if the monsters in the dark didn't exist.

"Excuse me?" she said.

With a beige coat, pixie haircut, and blue eyes, nothing distinguished her from a human woman at first glance. Yet the hunter's chocolate-brown eyes widened when he turned around, and his hands vanished into the pockets of his cognac-colored leather jacket, bringing a smile to her lips. He was not completely ignorant.

"Yes?" His body tensed.

"I've lost my way. Could you help me?" She held up a creased paper map. "Where exactly are we?"

He gaped at her obvious ruse before giving his head a quick shake. "Um…sure."

"Great!" Grinning, she closed the remaining distance between them.

After glancing at the map for less than a second, his eyes fixated on her again. "We're at the top left corner, at Forty-Seventh Avenue and Geary Boulevard."

"Guess I'm right where I should be." She leaned in close to whisper into his ear. "Thank you."

Her pulse quickened when she inhaled his scent. A stimulating mixture of orange, lavender, and sandalwood tempted her senses, and her mouth watered. Licking her lips, she let her head sink close to his neck. Her stomach constricted, and the beast in her roared for a taste. Her thin thread of control threatened to snap because she'd starved herself for too long again. What if she surrendered to the temptation?

His heartbeat hammered in her ears. Or was it hers? Her mouth was less than an inch from his neck, and nothing kept her from relinquishing control to the hated monster inside of her. *Just a little taste.*

Before she could sink her fangs into his skin, something pierced hers, and a horrible burning spread from her neck through her body. Only one thing caused such pain to a vampire.

"Silver," she hissed.

Clutching her neck, she put some distance between herself and the hunter.

A dark smile spread across his face as he put a syringe back into his coat pocket. "Silver nitrate, to be exact, blended with a strong tranquilizer."

She gulped. Drugs didn't have any effect on a vampire. But if they combined them with silver nitrate, all bets were off. While she didn't mind losing her false freedom, falling asleep during battle might cost her life. A slight dizziness already clouded her senses. Should she play it safe and run? *No.* Sticking to her plan trumped her survival. Being incapacitated even played into her hands.

The hunter drew his handgun and aimed it at her. "And if the drug doesn't bring you down, a silver bullet will. Permanently."

Despite the throbbing in her head, she grinned.

"Huh. I've underestimated you. But I'm not here to fight."

"You could have fooled me." He narrowed his eyes.

"Why? I'm unarmed."

"Except for your fangs." He scoffed. "Did you expect me to stand by while you turn me into your next meal?"

No, and I'm glad you didn't. She was in control for the moment. How long till hunger consumed her again? She shuddered. "It's in my nature to drink blood. I didn't *choose* this life."

"Neither did I. But I choose to protect others from your kind."

"As do I."

His head flinched back slightly, and he opened his mouth to speak.

The rest of his team—a tall man in a casual suit with short, black hair and a mustache, a chubby one with blond hair, wearing sweatpants, and a woman—raced toward them with their weapons drawn, encircling her.

Shit. She'd hoped for more time to talk.

The female hunter brushed her shoulder-length, dark-brown hair out of her face. "You picked the wrong target tonight!"

While the woman and the tall man carried a sword, the man in the sweatpants held a dagger in one hand and a silver-coated net in the other. They drew nearer, looking for an opening to attack.

With a heavy sigh, she raised her hands and kneeled down before the situation escalated. "I surrender."

Her eyelids grew heavy with fatigue, and she struggled to keep her eyes focused on the hunter with the gun.

His brows furrowed as he studied her. His gun never wavered.

"Secure her," he ordered.

She didn't defend herself when the tall hunter came from behind, pressed her into the asphalt, and cuffed her hands behind her back. When the silver handcuffs gnawed into her flesh, she grimaced.

"…not necessary," she mumbled as the chubby hunter threw his net on her.

Even if she'd wanted to resist, the pain from the silver nitrate combined with the drug already subdued her. Without fresh blood, her body lacked the energy to fight any longer. She was at the hunters' mercy.

Smiling, she welcomed the relief sleep offered.

****

Dave exhaled slowly to calm his racing heart. After holstering his gun, he studied the sleeping vampire with a frown. "Is it just me, or was subduing her a little too easy?"

"Don't worry so much." Emily smiled at him. "You were fantastic."

He rolled his eyes at her uncalled-for compliment. Yes, he'd rid the world of one more vampire, but in the grand scheme of things, her capture barely made a difference. Still, he'd continue to fight, just like his colleagues. And he wouldn't stop until all humans were safe from these creatures or he took his last breath. Although the latter would most likely come first, especially if he kept playing the bait. Speaking of which…"Why did she hesitate?"

Aaron sheathed his sword. "What are you talking about?"

"I thought she'd bite me, but she hesitated long

enough for me to drug her."

"Don't overthink her actions," Charles said. "I bet she wanted to savor your taste and took her time since she didn't expect to run into a hunter."

"Didn't she? Her behavior and her words felt off."

Charles shrugged. He fetched an apple from his backpack and cut into it with his silver dagger. Dave didn't bother telling him not to use his weapon as cutlery. Again.

"Why don't you interrogate her once she wakes?" Aaron said. "Let's bring her to the compound before a passerby notices us. I'll get the car."

"Okay, thanks." Dave kneeled to inspect the vampire's heart-shaped face through the silver net. Her blonde hair combined with her slim nose reminded him of his first girlfriend. The soft smile on her lips added to her allure. If not for her unnaturally pale skin tone, he'd call her delicate features charming. Still, her simple beauty stirred something deep inside him. *It's a pity she's a monster.*

Chapter 2

Gnawing hunger woke Sarah from a restless sleep. Her throat was dry, and her intestines hurt. The silver nitrate flowing through her veins intensified her misery, causing her blood to bubble and burn inside of her. The pain almost distracted her from the cold energy-sapping metal around her neck and wrists—a collar and manacles? With a groan, she opened her eyes to take in her surroundings.

Silver-coated bars and a locked cell door separated her from a corridor. Stone walls enclosed the other three sides of the six-foot-square small room in which she lay on a cold stone platform, serving as a bed without a mattress or bedding. The lack of comfort didn't faze her, because she'd spent most of her childhood without even basic amenities. Monsters like her required little to survive.

Two long silver chains connected the collar around her neck and the manacles to the wall behind her, giving her enough space to sit.

The sensible part of her brain told her everything was going according to plan—even if getting caught to help the hunters was a shitty plan. And yet her breathing quickened as panic built inside her chest. The cell was too small and too dark.

Her instincts screamed at her to flee. Pulling on the chains only caused the silver manacles to cut into her flesh, eliciting a whimper. The lack of fresh blood left her weak, unable to break free.

Closing her eyes, she thought back to her mother reading her bedtime stories. Her favorite one was a fairy tale about a boy who set out to learn fear. Remembering his brazen courage when faced with precarious situations helped her survive the horrors of captivity as a child. Even though she was the monster now, it still worked. Her heartbeat and breathing slowed while she recited the boy's journey in her mind.

After calming herself, she checked her body and clothes. She still wore the same white shirt and blue jeans, but her coat and boots were missing. Since they weren't hers to begin with, she had no right to complain. The face of the poor woman whose clothes she wore crossed her mind. *She can't use them anymore either...*

Clasping her knees to her chest, she curled up into a ball. *At least I can't hurt anyone else as long as I'm in here.*

****

The clock on his office wall ticked the seconds away as Dave filled out the last of the forms on his wooden desk. With a sigh, he leaned back in his chair. If he'd slain the vampire instead of bringing her in, he could have saved himself some paperwork and granted her a quick death. On the other hand, having her here gave him an opportunity to satisfy his curiosity about her weird behavior. Ian's experiments would kill her soon enough, sparing him the gruesome deed.

"Are you done for tonight?" Leaning against the doorframe to his office, Emily shot him a flirty grin. She'd changed into shorts and a low-cut V-neck tee, emphasizing her ample cleavage. "How about joining me on a late-night jog?"

He rolled his eyes at her provocative outfit. Her efforts to gain his attention were wasted since he didn't date colleagues. They risked their lives daily, and he wouldn't survive the death of another lover—the last one nearly broke him. Although they'd discussed his feelings years ago and she'd moved on, she never ceased her playful flirting.

Returning her grin, he said, "Not tonight, thanks. I still need to interview our new test subject. Have fun, though."

"You're all work and no play." She pouted and sighed dramatically. "Well, if you prefer the company of a bloodsucker, it's your loss." Her hips swayed with every step as she turned around and left.

It was no loss if he learned something helpful from the pretty mystery downstairs. Somehow, the prospect of her company intrigued him more than Emily's. He snorted at his abstruse thoughts while sorting the forms into a new case file labeled "Test Subject 057."

After taking the last sip of his coffee, he grabbed his smartphone and made his way to the southern dungeon. He unlocked the heavy door with a key from a hook on the wall, pushed it open, turned on the light, and walked down six steps to the first cell.

The vampire perched on the edge of the bed, and her eyes lit up with recognition. She watched him closely while he opened the voice recorder app on his phone, pressed play, and put the device on the ground between them.

"I've never seen a vampire surrender so easily," he said.

"I'm not your enemy, and I've got no reason to fight

9

you."

If only that were true. He uttered a brief laugh. "You're a vampire. I'm a hunter. We're natural enemies. What did you think would happen if you tried to feed on me? And don't tell me you didn't realize what I am."

She pursed her lips. "What makes you think I did?"

"You took your damn time trying to drain me…as if you didn't really want to." He frowned at the crazy notion.

She chuckled. "You're right. I didn't want to attack you…but not because you're a hunter. I hate being a vampire, feeding on humans, and the constant struggle of my dark urges versus my sense of what's right and what's wrong. Unfortunately, the hunger in me wins most of the time."

A pretty vampire with a conscience, huh? Interesting.

"Speaking of hunger, I haven't fed in days." She rubbed her stomach in soothing circles. "My insides are screaming for blood. Could you please get me some?"

"What do you think this is? A bar where you can trick the patrons into buying drinks for you?" He crossed his arms and raised his eyebrows. "In case you haven't realized it yet, you're our prisoner. As a hunter, it's my job to kill you, not to make you comfortable."

She gulped and slid back farther on the bed. "Well…you haven't killed me yet. So, I was hoping you needed something from me. Information maybe? I'm willing to cooperate."

Her small body seemed extremely fragile, and her frail-sounding voice awakened an urge in him to protect her. How would it feel to hold her close and comfort her? He balled his fists to smother his misplaced feelings of sympathy. "We can get all the information we need, regardless of whether you cooperate. You must be aware you're not getting out of here alive."

"I...I don't care. I just want to help." When her large, round eyes met his, he saw no deceit in them.

"Why?"

"Do you think I enjoy being a vampire? I never asked for this life, and I despise every second." Her body trembled, and she moaned. "This accursed hunger is making me crazy, and it goes against my nature to hurt and feed from people. So, I like the idea of helping those who fight against the monsters who turned me."

"Just because you're the enemy of our enemy doesn't make you our friend. All vampires need to be exterminated, and we don't make exceptions for pretty girls." Part of him detested watching her suffer. If only there were peaceful options to coexist. He ran his hand through his hair. His soft-heartedness would get him killed one day. "What did you hope to achieve here? Did you think we'd let you walk if you told us you hated your own kind?"

"No." She bit her lip. "You don't have to let me walk. But I truly wish to help."

Yeah, right. "So, you expect me to believe you don't care about your freedom?"

"I've never been free, and I never will be." Her breathing turned ragged. "I'm a slave to my instincts and the thirst for blood. At least I can't hurt innocent people while I'm in here."

What a load of bullshit, but she's chatty. "Since you're more civil and talkative than most, you'll get the chance to prove your usefulness."

"Thank you," she said with a pained smile. The

thirst was taking a toll on her.

What distinguished humans from these monsters, if not their compassion? Even if these creatures in human bodies deserved pain, suffering, and death, he persisted in treating them humanely. With a sigh, he left the dungeon to fetch blood bags.

The large community kitchen looked empty. Only the medical refrigerator buzzed loudly. He opened it to take two bags of blood they keep for their test subjects. Once he closed the door and turned to leave, a tantalizing smell greeted him from the coffee machine. While blood wouldn't get cold, the fresh coffee would, so he grabbed a small cup and filled it with the delicious beverage.

After taking a few sips, he spotted a teddy bear lying on the ground. With a knowing smile, he put the cup on the kitchen table and bent down to pick up the soft, plush toy. "What are you doing here all alone, Mister Bear?"

"He's not alone," a meek voice whispered from below the table.

"Oh?" He crouched down to come face-to-face with two kids in their pajamas. "Shouldn't you be in bed? And where's Anthony?"

"He's asleep. But we couldn't sleep," Lily said.

"You didn't tell us a bedtime story tonight, Uncle Dave," Tim explained.

"I didn't, did I? Sorry, I was busy working." He scratched his neck. "It's no excuse for you to be up this late, though."

"Sorry," the two said in unison, looking down sheepishly.

"Why don't you go back to bed now, and I'll check on you once I'm done with work?" With a smile, he handed Lily her teddy.

"All right," Tim said. "See you later, Uncle Dave."

He followed the kids until they reached the stairs. Satisfied they'd find their way back to their dorm, he returned to the dungeon.

In her cell, the vampire was rocking back and forth on the bed.

"Catch." He tossed a bag through the bars.

With reflexes fast as lightning, she grabbed it, brought it to her lips, and bit into the plastic with her fangs. Once the liquid entered her body, she sagged against the wall with a moan.

He wrinkled his nose. *Disgusting.*

After less than a minute, she'd emptied the contents of the bag and tossed it back at him.

"Thank you." Her voice was heavy with emotion.

"Don't get used to it. I wanted to keep you talking, but the hunger seemed to distract you too much."

She nodded. "Regular blood consumption is vital to me because I'm still young. Since I loathe feeding on humans, I often starve myself. After a while, it hurts so much I can't think straight."

"How old are you? You don't look any older than eighteen or nineteen."

"I *am* eighteen years old," she said. "Have been for over six months now—which is also the time I've been a vampire."

His eyes widened. If she was telling the truth, she was four years younger than him. "Even though you're hurting for blood, you seem in control. In my experience, young vampires react much stronger to silver or being starved."

She avoided his gaze. "I've been through a lot. Even before they turned me, vampires tortured me for years.

13

So, I learned to endure pain."

He swallowed with difficulty as his throat tightened. "I can see where your hatred for your own kind stems from."

"Why do you hate vampires?" she asked.

His mind traveled back to the night it started.

Six and a half years ago, he'd been out celebrating with his friends and came home past his curfew with his girlfriend Maya in tow. While he fetched his guitar from the trunk, she danced on the lawn, giggling. Her red dress and black hair swirled as she spun around.

"Quiet," he whispered on the way to the front door.

She shrugged. "The light is on, anyway."

He sighed and pulled his keys out of his pants pocket. When he arrived at the entrance, he froze. "Why's the door ajar?"

"They're probably expecting us." She pushed the door all the way open and entered.

He followed her inside and closed it behind them.

A scream tore through the night. He turned around to see Maya standing in the living room, her mouth agape.

"What's wrong?" He hurried to her side, and chills traveled down his body.

The large TV lay toppled on the floor. Pieces of broken glass, his Blu-ray collection, and flowerpots littered the floor. Splatters of blood glistened in the artificial light. His legs gave in when he spotted the lifeless body of his mother on the couch.

"There's our dessert," a cheerful voice had said from the hallway.

He shook his head to rid himself of the memory. "It's none of your business." His lips still quivered.

A part of him had died that night. And no matter how many vampires he killed for revenge, the hollow feeling inside of him only grew. At least he was protecting others from the same fate.

"I'm sorry," she whispered.

Without another word, he picked up his phone, stopped the recording, and tossed her the second bag of blood.

He hadn't reminisced about his past in months. Had her slight resemblance to Maya triggered the flashback? Drowning the memories with the bottle of rum Aaron had given him for his birthday sounded incredibly tempting. It was time to call it a day.

Chapter 3

After a good day's rest and enough time for the second bag of blood to do its healing magic, the silver nitrate had dissolved, and Sarah felt much better, her gnawing hunger satiated for the time being. Even the silver collar and manacles didn't faze her any longer.

With a clear mind, she inspected her cell more closely. An electric lantern hanging on the corridor wall illuminated her surroundings, soothing her nerves. Despite being a creature of the night with excellent vision, she despised the dark. Nothing good ever happened in places untouched by light.

Claw marks graced the walls, and the foul stench of dried blood reached her sensitive nose. How many vampires had died in this place? Would she become nothing but a stain on the wall as well? She shivered.

After shaking the dreary thought from her head, she concentrated on nearby sounds. Although dozens of feet shuffled on the ground beyond the door and above her head, no one headed her way. She was all alone.

She picked up the empty bag and stared at it. Drinking bagged blood didn't compare with drinking from a human. The liquid was cold and less vibrant, and the taste nauseated her. Nevertheless, it satisfied her hunger while putting no one at risk, which was what she'd hoped for. Would they continue feeding her? And what were her options if they didn't?

Lost in thoughts, she fumbled with the bag until the hallway door opened with a groan. The hunter from the previous night walked down the stairs to her cell, followed by a man in his early forties with glasses, dark hair, and a white lab coat, holding a clipboard in his hands.

She straightened up and smiled at them. "Good morning. Or evening, depending on when you got up. Or let's settle on hello."

The older man flinched, causing her to frown.

"I warned you she was chattier than most." The hunter smirked.

"What can I do for you?" she asked him.

"I'm here for security reasons." He gestured toward the gun at his belt and then toward the older man. "This is Dr. Ian Crowley, the head of our Vampire Research Department. He wants to ask you some questions to further his research."

Dr. Crowley raised his hand in greeting.

"You study us? Cool." She leaned toward him and tilted her head. "Then you must work with a lot of vampires. Why did my greeting startle you?"

His eyes darted to the ground. "We usually drug our test subjects."

Oh. So, he never talks to them...

"Dr. Crowley develops weapons for us," the hunter explained.

"Did you create the silver nitrate drug?" she asked the scientist.

He nodded.

"Impressive."

"Um, thanks." He blushed. "So...Test Subject 057, what can you tell me about—"

"I've got a name."

He blinked at her. "What?"

It's not like it matters, but still... "My name is Sarah."

"Okay, um…S-Sarah." He stared at her as if slowly absorbing her words.

"Yes?"

He cleared his throat. "We've already collected information on vampires, but it's mostly experimental data. I'd like you to tell me all about your kind so we can verify our theories."

"Sure. What would you like to know?"

"Well…could you tell me something about a vampire's weaknesses?"

"You already know the most important one—silver. It represses our abilities, slows our healing, and thus makes us more prone to die. Staking a vampire's heart with a silver weapon or piercing it with silver bullets means almost certain death. So does cutting our heads off, with or without silver." She waited while Dr. Crowley took notes. "Another well-known weakness is sunlight, although it's not deadly."

"Not even to older vampires?" He looked up from his clipboard.

"No, it simply weakens us and sometimes causes an allergic reaction. Why would you think otherwise?"

"I saw a vampire die at sunrise," the hunter said.

"Did you really?" she asked. "Or did he fool you?"

"How could he? When the rays of the sun touched his body, he screamed and dissolved into thin air."

"Sorry to burst your bubble. He didn't dissolve. He most likely teleported somewhere." She chuckled. She had so much to teach them.

"So, you can actually teleport?" Dr. Crowley's eyes sparkled. "Although we assumed some vampires possessed such an ability, we've found no evidence."

"*I* can't." *Probably.* At least she never learned how to. "But teleportation is a common skill among more experienced vampires."

"What other special abilities do vampires possess?" Dr. Crowley asked.

"Apart from supernatural speed and strength? It differs for every vampire. Some of us can read your mind or control your actions, for example."

The hunter stiffened. "Can you?"

She shook her head. "No, I'm too young. As far as I know, those abilities take decades or centuries to emerge."

"Back to your weaknesses, then." Dr. Crowley clicked his ballpoint pen twice. "How about poison, fire, or suffocation? Would those things kill you?"

She scratched her chin. "Most poisons don't kill or even affect vampires. I wouldn't bet my life on it, though. There are so many substances and combinations thereof, like your clever mix of silver nitrate with the tranquilizer. Fire wouldn't kill me unless I'm completely reduced to ashes. And I doubt I could suffocate since I don't *need* to breathe to survive. Breathing is merely a habit and useful for regulating my emotions and taking in scents. The only thing a vampire requires is blood."

"Would you die if we starved you?" the hunter asked.

She frowned. Their line of questioning was taking an unpleasant turn. "No. I'd end up in a death-like state and reawaken once someone fed me fresh blood."

"Fascinating." Dr. Crowley leaned closer to her, and

a whiff of vanilla and almonds mixed with chemicals reached her nose. Sweet, but not as tantalizing as the hunter's scent. "I think I'd like to test that sometime."

Not with me, hopefully. She pressed her lips into a thin line and scooted farther away. Helping them was one thing, allowing them to torture her quite another.

The hunter nudged him in the ribs. "I'm sure we've got less forthcoming vampires to study starvation on."

"Oh, yes, of course." Dr. Crowley straightened his glasses. "Although there are a bunch of tests I'd love to run on her."

She narrowed her eyes at them. "As long as it's nothing unnecessarily painful, I'll cooperate in your experiments." Hell, as long as they didn't cripple or kill her, she'd do anything to help them learn more about exterminating her damned species.

"Perfect." A wide smile built on the doctor's lips. He nodded toward the hunter and left.

"All right," the hunter said. "Since Dr. Crowley needs to prepare his experiments, we're done for tonight. Do you require another bag of blood?"

"Yes, please. Because of my age, I should feed daily." Especially when so many mouth-watering humans surrounded her.

"As long as you're cooperating, I'm sure we can accommodate this need," the hunter said on his way upstairs.

Half an hour later, he brought her some blood.

"How about telling me your name?" she asked before piercing the bag with her fangs.

The hunter grimaced as he watched her drink.

Once she'd emptied the bag, she tilted her head. "Well?"

"Most hunters have lost someone or suffered at the hands of vampires, so we can never be friends, you know?"

She felt a sting in her chest at his words. "I'd still like to know your name."

He sighed. "Dave."

"Nice to meet you, Dave." She smiled. "And thank you so much for the blood."

He didn't respond.

Chapter 4

The next evening, Dave asked Charles and Aaron to accompany him to the vampire's holding cell. They put on their black, reinforced uniforms and armed themselves.

"Tranquilizing her would be much easier," Aaron said on the way down.

"Yes," Dave agreed, "but then we'd rob Ian of the chance to experiment on a mostly willing participant. At least for now, let's play along with her games to benefit from her talkativeness. Besides, a young vampire like her can't put up much of a fight."

Aaron shrugged. "It's your call."

They fell silent as Dave opened the door to the dungeon and descended the stairs.

The vampire winced once they came into view. Her eyes grew large at their sight, and her face turned even paler than its usual ivory tone.

"We're here to take you to Dr. Crowley's lab," he said, and she visibly relaxed. "As long as you behave, we won't have to hurt or sedate you."

"I understand," she said.

Aaron and Charles trained their guns on her as Dave entered the cell. Her eyes followed his every move as he approached, put a helmet on her head—one of Ian's inventions—and locked it with a tiny key. With a silver-coated mesh in front, it resembled a fencing mask, preventing her from biting anyone.

Next, he unlocked the two chains connecting her to the wall and attached a new, shorter one to her manacles. She sucked in a small breath when his hand brushed the back of hers by accident. He searched her eyes for the cause of her reaction, but she glanced away.

When he pulled on his end of the chain, she got up.

He led her out of the cell, up the stairs, through the large main hall, and down the long white corridors to the laboratory. After several turns, they arrived at the glass entrance, which opened when he put his electronic key card to the sensor next to the door.

A slight chill traveled down his body as they entered the lab. With glaring lights, white tiles, and interior windows for observation, everything looked sterile and too similar to a hospital. The sight aroused too many memories of the long hours he'd spent in intensive care, fighting for his life. His first encounter with vampires and learning about the deaths of his family and girlfriend had shaken him to the core. After all these years, the anguish still choked him.

Books and binders full of notes filled shelves and cabinets at the far end of the room. Laptops, electronic devices, chemical substances, and various tools lay on four large desks, and an apparatus that looked like something between a dental and an electric chair stood in the center.

The vampire swallowed hard when he asked her to sit in the chair. Yet she obeyed. Even when he tied her arms, legs, neck, and upper body to the apparatus, she didn't struggle or protest. Did she possess no sense of self-preservation? Or did the guns of his colleagues frighten her enough to keep her docile?

He checked the restraints once more before removing the helmet. "You okay?"

She pressed her lips together and nodded.

"Good. Dr. Crowley will be with you momentarily. If you acquit yourself well, you'll get a bag of blood afterward."

"There she is!" Ian entered the lab, followed by his assistants.

Dave nodded toward them in greeting. "I'll wait outside if you need me."

He left the lab and lodged himself in a chair, monitoring the vampire through one of the interior windows. Part of him wondered if he was supposed to protect the scientists from her or the vampire from Ian's enthusiasm.

****

"Could you eat this?" Dr. Crowley's female assistant showed Sarah a plate of garlic cloves.

She rolled her eyes. In the past hours, she'd already undergone a long list of medical examinations, answered questions, and taken part in countless experiments. While she applauded their thoroughness, this was getting ridiculous. "Garlic doesn't deter me. But I don't eat anymore."

"Are you physically capable of eating?" Dr. Crowley asked.

"I guess so. My body can't digest anything. Yet I can chew and swallow food, and it'll dissolve once I drink blood."

"What does it have to do with blood? What effects does it have on you?" the assistant asked.

"Blood does not simply quench my hunger. It heals and rids my body of any damaging or unnecessary substances like poison, silver, and edibles. If I eat something, my body requires more blood afterward. Since vampires don't enjoy the taste of food, there's usually no reason for us to consume it."

"Will you humor us and eat a clove of garlic, anyway?"

Sarah arched an eyebrow. "Even you wouldn't eat a raw clove of garlic, would you?"

When a flush appeared on the woman's face, she added, "But sure, I'll do it. Can't taste worse than any other food."

She opened her mouth and waited for the assistant to put the clove on her tongue with barbecue tongs. After chewing a few times, she gulped it down with a grimace. "Satisfied?"

It didn't taste as bad as she remembered—as a child, she once bit into a large piece of garlic her big brother had hidden in the candy jar as a prank.

"Yes, thank you," Dr. Crowley said. "Now, how about religion?"

His other assistant, a slender old man, picked up a crucifix and a dusty Bible from a nearby shelf. "Do these items affect you?"

"No." She stifled a laugh. "I'm sure you want to confirm my answer. So, go ahead."

The assistant's face fell when she didn't shriek from the cross or his recitation of the Old Testament. She watched his efforts with amusement.

"All right." Dr. Crowley cleared his throat. "We're almost done for today. On your way back to the cell, I'd like to test your claim regarding the effect of sunlight. The sun rose about half an hour ago—time flies when you're having fun." He chuckled. "Anyway, you mentioned getting an allergic reaction from sunlight. How bad would that be?"

"I'm not sure because I haven't been outside in the daytime since becoming a vampire. As far as I know, the sun will weaken me mentally, and I might develop a rash. The effects will fade once I drink blood. So, I'll be fine." Her heart jumped with excitement at the prospect of seeing the light of day again. Even as a human, she rarely got to see the blue sky.

The lab door opened, and Dave and the other two hunters entered. While Dave prepared her for the transport, Dr. Crowley instructed him to take a detour through the garden.

He turned to her with a frown. "Will you be fine in the sun?"

"Probably." She laughed sheepishly. Did he worry about her?

After putting the helmet back on her head and freeing her from the chair, he led her outside, followed by the other hunters and Dr. Crowley.

They took a few different turns and ended up in an inner courtyard.

Sparrows chirped excitedly, and the fruity scent of exotic flowers filled the air. The cocktail of flavors ensnared her senses, and the memory of drinking a glass of the multivitamin juice her mum used to buy entered her mind. To her, it would never taste the same again.

Everything was bright. Much too bright. And yet, the garden's beauty awed her.

On one side, multicolored flowerbeds in red, pink, white, and yellow surrounded two wooden benches with names carved into the backrest. On the other side, a sandstone water fountain spouted water, which trickled down three tiers into a koi pond. It was a paradise for humans to escape into, where they could forget about monsters like her. She didn't belong in this peaceful image.

When the skin of her bare arms prickled, she looked up to see the sun peeking through the clouds. She squinted her eyes from the gleaming light, which burned her irises through the mesh of her helmet.

"Are you okay?" Dave asked.

She blinked. "Yeah. I shouldn't look at the sun."

"I was talking about the red spots covering your arms."

"They itch a little, but it's not bad. Besides, the garden is gorgeous."

"You're not here to enjoy the view."

"Sorry." Her head dropped, and her eyes sank to the ground. A monster like her didn't deserve to look at beautiful things.

He sighed. "Let's get you inside."

Five minutes later, he chained her to the wall of her cell again. After removing her helmet and locking her door, he left while the scientist and the other two hunters stayed behind.

Dr. Crowley inspected her rash from the other side of the bars. "The reaction was less severe than I expected. How are you feeling?"

"Okay. My arms are still itching, though."

"How long until they heal?"

"Depends." She nibbled on her lips. "If you give me blood, you can watch the rash disappear."

Dave's chuckle sounded from the top of the stairs as he returned with a bag of blood in his hands. "Are you trying to give us reasons to feed you?"

She shrugged. "I'm just stating a fact."

He tossed her the bag. "Well then, show us your regenerative powers."

The moment the blood entered her system, the itching stopped. She closed her eyes for a second to revel in the pleasure washing through her. When she opened them again, Dr. Crowley gaped at her arms. The rash had vanished.

"I told you blood had a powerful effect on us." She smiled.

Dr. Crowley simply nodded. A moment later, he mumbled something about further research and left. The hunters followed him.

Chapter 5

Dave's mind wandered to the vampire in the dungeon while he tossed and turned in bed. Did she truly intend to help them? What had she endured to turn on her own kind? A helpless human growing up among beasts feasting on her blood…his heart ached for the girl who hadn't had a chance at life. But she was a monster now. With a groan, he shook her image from his head. Why was he even thinking about her?

The clock on his nightstand read 5:22 p.m. Less than one hour until his alarm went off. Most hunters adapted and turned their nights into days because vampire sightings usually happened after dark. Maintaining an inverted sleep schedule had its drawbacks. He missed the most random things—wearing sunglasses outside, meeting friends for volleyball and ice cream at the beach, or watching hummingbirds dive through the air. They all sacrificed so much to ensure the safety of normal people.

Since sleep eluded him, he could just as well revel in the remaining sunlight. He stretched and rolled out of bed. After putting on a tracksuit, he went for a run.

When he returned an hour later, he took a long shower before making his way to the community kitchen. His team members huddled around a round table, browsing through a report while eating breakfast.

"Morning." Emily smiled at him. "We've got a case."

"We do?" He raised his brows. As team lead, it was his duty to coordinate with management and present new cases to his colleagues.

"I ran into Peter while he was searching for you. Since you weren't here, he gave me the information," Aaron explained.

A glance at the wall clock revealed it was thirty minutes past their usual meeting time. He rubbed his temple. Maybe caffeine would put him back on track. "Thanks. Let me grab a coffee. I'll be right with you."

With a hot drink and a bowl of granola with milk and berries, he joined his teammates at the table. Since a large map with several red marks took up most of the space, he didn't put his bowl down.

"Another one in San Francisco," Aaron explained. "We've already marked presumed killings and sightings on the map."

"Fisherman's Wharf, huh?" He gulped down a big spoon full of granola. "We have to be careful not to cause a scene with tourists around."

"The vamp's already causing a scene," Charles said, chewing on a toast. "Several tourists went missing. Since the police discovered one of them drained of blood near the piers two days ago, they're patrolling the area."

"Peter made some calls earlier. They know we're coming and won't bother us," Emily said.

"Good. Let's not waste time then. Meet me at the car in fifteen minutes." He swallowed three more spoons of breakfast before disposing of the leftovers. With his coffee in hand, he hurried to his room to get his equipment.

****

Even after dark, hundreds of people frequented the

colorful shops, attractions, and restaurants at Pier 39. Lights illuminated most of the two-story outdoor mall, giving unsuspecting tourists a wrong sense of safety.

"Let's split up," Dave said. "Don't forget to call for backup if you spot the vampire."

Aaron, Charles, and Emily nodded before setting off in different directions.

He meandered through the area until whining and grunts near the end of the pier drew his attention. A chill crept down his spine, and he ran toward the sound, his hand reaching for his phone. Once he spotted the source of the noises, he relaxed. Dozens of sea lions lounged on wooden platforms or piled on top of each other. He chuckled at himself as he watched two of them bicker. How could he forget about this popular tourist attraction? He'd even visited this place a couple of times with his parents.

He turned around to check the shops and restaurants again. As he passed the nostalgic San Francisco carousel, a shadow moved between the artistically crafted mounts. Or did the lights play tricks on his mind? He approached to get a better look.

Since it was after hours, no one should be on the ride. Yet something moved on the ground, behind an oversized rabbit mount. A dark-haired man in a black coat bent over a woman, pressing her to the ground. The woman moaned. Was it from pleasure or pain? After taking a few more steps, he shone his phone's flashlight in their direction just as the man buried his face in the girl's throat. *Vampire!*

He drew his sword. "Get away from her!"

Blood dripped down the vampire's face as he glanced up.

What a beast! He's nothing like her. He stilled at his thought. Why was the female vampire on his mind again?

The vampire licked his lips. "Do you fancy taking her place?"

"As if." Dave spit on the ground. "I'll send you to your grave instead."

The vampire got to his feet with a wide smile on his lips. "You really think you'd stand a chance against me?"

"I eat trash like you for breakfast."

"Oh, yeah?" The vampire charged at him. With a fast, pointed kick to Dave's sword arm, he disarmed him.

Dave groaned as pain seared through his shoulder. His weapon clattered a few feet to his right. He had no time to pick it back up because the beast came at him again.

Their bodies collided, and they toppled to the ground, grappling. While Dave struggled against the vampire's brute strength, trying to keep him from his throat, they rolled into a hollow space below some stairs—away from sight.

Fuck. His breathing quickened, and he tried to wrestle free. But the vampire overpowered him, fixing his hands above his head. *Serves me right for forgetting to call for backup.*

"Seems like I'll be eating *you* tonight." The vampire lowered his head to Dave's throat. "I love the exquisite taste of young, naïve hunters."

Unable to break free, he shuddered beneath the monster. He cried out when the vampire's teeth pierced his skin. With every sip of blood, agonizing waves of pain flooded his body, and a terrible burning spread from the puncture wounds.

His heart thrashed in his chest. Even as he pushed against the beast with all his strength, his opponent didn't budge. And with every passing second, his body weakened.

An ear-splitting shot rang through the night.

With a hiss, the vampire released him. The beast's eyes bulged as blood spilled from a wound in his abdomen. He took one last look at Dave, and a malicious smirk spread across his face before he vanished.

When Dave attempted to sit up, his vision blurred, and he blacked out.

****

Beep…beep…beep…

Dave opened his eyes to find himself in a white room. The sun glared through a window with see-through curtains, yet he felt freezing cold. When his eyes fell on an intravenous drip and the monitor beeping next to him, he groaned. *I hate hospitals.*

A chair scraped against the floor, and Emily appeared at his side. "You're awake. Thank God!"

"What happened?" he asked.

"I should ask you the same question. Why'd you face the bloodsucker on your own?"

Because I was stupid. His head pounded as he tried to remember more details. "There was no time. He was feeding on a woman. Did you save her?"

She nodded. "I was nearby and heard you engage the vampire. When I came running, I noticed him dragging you into the darkness. I texted the others before approaching, though." She gave him a pointed look, and he winced. "As soon as I was close enough, I fired a shot. But the bastard disappeared before I could end him. Once the others arrived, we secured the area, sent the female victim to the hospital, took care of your wounds, and brought you back here."

"Thanks," he murmured. "So…what's my prognosis?"

"You've lost a lot of blood, and it looks like the vamp has given you an infection."

"An infection?" He drew his eyebrows up.

She squeezed her lips together. "You've got a fever. Ian is running tests on your blood to find out more."

"Shit." Other hunters had gotten infected from bites before. Most didn't make it.

"Anyway, I'll let Ian know you're awake." She squeezed his hand before leaving. "I'm sure you'll be fine." Her words lacked conviction.

Chapter 6

Based on the fragments of conversations beyond the door, it was day again, which meant no one had visited Sarah for over twenty-four hours. The beast in her screamed for blood, keeping her awake. She wrapped her trembling arms around her knees as her insides constricted in pain. The first hours of starvation were always excruciating. Would Dave remember to feed her soon? Her heart rate sped up at the thought of him. She could almost smell his fresh, spicy odor and imagine the taste of him on her tongue. Closing her eyes, she pictured licking the sensitive skin on his neck, searching for the perfect spot to bite. Would his blood be as tantalizing as his scent?

The door opened, and daylight illuminated the corridor, pulling her from her forbidden fantasies. She sat up as Dave staggered down the stairs, followed by Dr. Crowley. Beads of sweat coated Dave's forehead, and a foul stench penetrated her nose as he leaned against her cell door, panting.

"Are you okay?" she asked, forgetting her all-consuming hunger.

"As if you care about me, bloodsucker."

She winced. Why was he acting so hostile?

With shaking hands, he opened the cell door and approached her. He drew his gun and held it to her temple. "If you don't want to die right now, you'll tell me everything you know about vampire viruses."

Too close. Her heart drummed and the beast in her howled. *Blood.* Her eyes wandered to his neck. *Blood.* The liquid she craved was almost within her grasp. She only needed to lean forward to consume it. *Blood.* Her stomach lurched, and her thoughts twirled.

Blood. Blood. Blood. Nothing else mattered.

But she was here for a different reason, wasn't she?

She hissed at him and dug her nails into her skin to regain her focus. "Get. Away. From. Me."

He stared at her blankly.

"Dave, I think she's ravenous," Dr. Crowley said. "You might not get much from her in this state."

He backed off slowly and holstered his gun. Once he locked the door, she took a calming breath.

"He's right. You shouldn't approach me when I'm hungry."

"I shouldn't?" He scoffed. "What gives you the right to tell me what to do?"

It's for your own safety. She sighed, and a shudder coursed through her body. "Otherwise, I can't concentrate on anything except for blood…Makes it hard for me to focus on your questions." Her insides still ached for a taste, but she could suppress her urges as long as he kept his distance.

He leaned against the far wall, crossing his arms. "So…vampire viruses?"

"There's no such thing. Vampires don't get sick. Viruses can't reproduce or even survive in our bodies."

"Then how come I got infected?"

"What do you mean?" Her eyes widened in realization when he touched his neck. "Did a vampire bite you?"

He nodded.

She squeezed her lips together. "You're not sick. You were poisoned."

"Poisoned?" His sickly pale face blanched even more. "How?"

"How can you know so much about vampires and so little at the same time?" she said, mostly to herself.

He slammed his fist against the wall behind him, causing her to flinch. "Well, enlighten us."

"Like snakes, vampires have hollow fangs, acting like needles. So, when we bite a human, we can inject them with certain fluids."

"Fluids? To poison us?" Dr. Crowley asked while jotting down notes on his clipboard.

"Yes, although some serve a different purpose."

"Like what?"

"There is one to ease the pain of the bite, one to make it pleasurable, one to make our victims sleepy, one to make them fall unconscious, one to poison them, another one to immobilize them, and one to affect their short-term memories. Vampires often mix these fluids to achieve a desired effect. There is also one to prepare for the transformation of a human into a vampire."

"Can you produce those fluids at will?" Dr. Crowley asked.

She nodded. "While feeding on a victim, yes."

He scratched his chin. "Is there a way to extract them for study?"

"Not unless I bite someone."

Dave cleared his throat. "Back to the issue at hand. Is there an antidote to your venom?"

"There's no universal cure or anything since each vampire produces a unique substance. We can neutralize our own venom, though."

Dave rubbed his temple. "You're saying I can't get cured unless I get the antidote from the vampire who bit me?"

She glanced at Dr. Crowley. "How about you develop a cure?"

A flush crept across the scientist's cheeks. "I'm afraid we don't have the time, knowledge, or equipment."

"Are you saying I'm a lost cause?" Dave asked.

"Your body might fight it off on its own, but it's unlikely." She bit her lip while meeting his gaze. "Or I could inject you with my antidote. If we're lucky, it's close enough to the one you need."

"Inject me? You mean bite me?" He snorted. "You must be joking. As if I'd let you anywhere near my veins."

Her shoulders slumped. "I simply aim to help you."

"I'd rather die." His harsh words hurt more than the hunger raging in her.

"You might…If you change your mind, you know where to find me."

"Yeah, rotting in here." He turned toward the exit. "Let's go, Ian."

****

With unsteady feet, Dave headed for the kitchen, followed by Ian. He poured himself a cup of coffee before collapsing onto a chair. Despite the warm beverage in his hand, his whole body shivered.

"Do you believe her?" he asked.

"She's got no reason to lie about this. And poisoning explains why our antibiotics have never helped. With this knowledge, we can research new treatments."

"So, you *can* cure me?" He held his breath while waiting for the answer.

"We can run more tests and try common treatments, but don't get your hopes up. It may take years until we find an effective way to counter vampire venom."

Time he didn't have. He supported his pounding head with his left hand and squeezed his eyes shut for a second. "Which means I'll die."

Ian took a deep breath. "Possibly. We don't know how your body will handle the venom."

"If you were me, would you…" He trailed off. Was he honestly considering taking the vampire up on her offer? *These damn headaches are turning me nuts.* "Forget it."

"Would I let her bite me?" Ian guessed.

"I said forget it," he grumbled. It was her fault he got bitten. She'd distracted him. "We should get rid of her. One less bloodsucker to worry about."

Ian raised his brows. "Why? I'd love to study her more."

"Of course you do. Never mind my ramblings, I'm not feeling too good."

Ian put the back of his hand on Dave's forehead. "Your fever's getting worse. You better return to the hospital wing."

"I'm not spending my last days or hours in the hospital."

Ignoring Ian's protests, he pushed to his feet. The ground swayed as he made his way to the staircase and up to the kids' dorm room. Every step exhausted him, and the distance felt insurmountable. Yet he kept going, slowly putting one foot in front of the other, until he arrived.

Three pairs of eyes beamed at him as he opened the door.

"Uncle Dave!" Lily, Tim, and Anthony came running. "We missed you!"

Forcing a smile, he kneeled to return their hug. "I'm sorry I missed story-time last night."

"We'll forgive you," Anthony said smugly, "if you read us a super long story tonight."

"I'll see what I can do." Dave chuckled. "We can start right after you brush your teeth and put on your pj's."

"Okay!" The kids ran to the bathroom.

Not daring to stand up again because the world still spun around him, he crawled to the kids' beds and leaned against the biggest one. His eyes fell shut, and he dozed off.

"Are you okay?" Lily nudged him on his shoulder. "You're sweating so much."

"I…" He opened his eyes. How could he tell them he was fine if he might not survive the night? "No. I got poisoned."

"Poisoned?" Tim gaped at him. "Will you be fine?"

"Not sure…" His vision blurred, and he felt queasy. What was he even doing here? "Sorry, maybe reading is not a good idea."

"You should see the doctor," Anthony said.

"Please get better soon." Lily sniffed. "I don't want to lose you."

A shudder went through him. He could not die and make these kids suffer the loss of yet another person.

Chapter 7

Even though pangs of hunger kept her awake, Sarah had lost all appetite for blood. She still smelled the pungent odor of death surrounding Dave. The scent nauseated her.

With a moan, she curled up on the cold stone bed. The venom was too strong for his body to fight on its own, but she could not force him to accept her help.

She'd seen many humans die—some even by her hand when she'd lost control. And yet, her throat constricted at the thought of his impending death. Although he considered her an enemy, he treated her kindly most of the time, listened to her, and brought her blood. Who'd take his place if he didn't survive?

She loathed her helplessness to save him, but her only option was to hope for his return.

And he returned a few hours later. The tall hunter from his team accompanied Dave, supporting him as they plodded down the stairs to her cell.

"You got a cure for him?" the tall hunter asked.

She bit her bottom lip. "I do, although I don't know if it'll work."

"It better work," he said. "So, what is it?"

"I'll have to bite him."

His mouth fell open. "You can't seriously consider this, Dave!"

"Aaron, please." Dave groaned. Sweat covered his

41

body, and he rasped for air. "I'm dying, so what's the harm in giving it a shot?"

Aaron sighed. "What do we have to do?"

"First, I need blood. Lots of blood," she said. "Otherwise, I risk killing him by accident because I haven't fed."

Aaron glanced at Dave, who nodded. He leaned him against the wall. "I'll be right back."

Unable to stay on his feet with no one supporting him, Dave sank to the ground.

Her first impulse was to hurry to his side, to embrace, and to comfort him. Yet the bars stopped her from giving in to the unusual yearning. She completely dismissed it once Aaron returned with three bags of blood and handed them to her.

The tall hunter curled his lips in disgust while she stilled her hunger. The blood didn't appeal much to her either since it tasted like ashes. Yet its nutritional value sufficed to drown the hungry beast in her. Three bags were more than what her body required, but she emptied them to stifle any inhuman urges.

"You can bring him to me now," she said once she'd gulped down the last drop.

After another glance at Dave, Aaron opened the cell door. "Don't move." He carried Dave inside and put him next to her on the stone bed before locking both of them in. "If he dies, so do you."

She nodded absentmindedly. His threats meant little to her when Dave was hanging on to life by a thread. The stink of death overshadowed his aromatic scent. His eyes were closed, and he was barely conscious.

Her stomach churned. He was so close—close enough to touch. When she brushed a few stray hairs out of his face, he shivered. His skin felt hot and sweaty. He panted for air. His body was fighting to keep him alive. Could she truly save him with her cursed powers, or would her bite worsen his state? There was only one way to find out.

She climbed atop his body—as far as the chains binding her allowed—to get better access to his neck. Her heart leaped in her chest when he trembled beneath her. Was he scared of her or a looming death?

"Relax," she whispered. "You'll be fine."

Slowly, she let her fangs sink down to his throat, bracing herself. As soon as she pierced his skin, she willed him to feel no pain. A small sip of blood revealed what she already knew—his body was losing the fight against the venom. The bitter fluid in his veins tainted the taste, but she didn't intend to feed, anyway. Instead, she concentrated on injecting him with as much of her antidote as possible.

"All done," she announced a minute later. "I hope it didn't hurt too badly?"

His eyes fluttered open, and he met her gaze. "Not at all…Your bite soothed the pain in my head."

"Good." With a smile, she pricked her index finger on a fang and smeared the building drop of blood onto her bite mark. Another idea formed in her head as his skin healed. "I don't know if my antidote suffices to fight the venom, but there's another method to improve your chances."

His lips parted slightly. "I'll do anything."

"Great! Remember that attitude because this will taste gross." She bit into her wrist before offering it to him. "Drink."

He wrinkled his nose, yet he leaned forward to

accept the blood. The click of a gun stopped them.

"You're not thinking of turning him into a monster right under our noses, are you?" Aaron asked, aiming his weapon at her.

"What?" Dave stiffened.

She rolled her eyes. "It doesn't work like that, I promise. Our blood possesses healing properties, which will help against the venom."

"And we're just supposed to trust your words?" Aaron asked.

"I believe you," Dave said, ignoring his colleague.

Her heart cartwheeled as his words sank in. He *trusted* her.

He closed his mouth around her wrist and gulped the blood down with a grimace.

Having him suck her blood was the strangest sensation. Something deep in her core tingled at the feel of his lips on her skin, and a moan escaped her. She almost protested when he released her wrist because the wound had healed.

When she gazed into his eyes, a flame burned in them, giving him new life, and color returned to his cheeks.

She quickly glanced away before giving in to the desire to run her hands along his skin to reassure herself his fever was decreasing. She cleared her throat. "Now it's up to your immune system. You better let your doctors monitor your vitals, though."

****

Ian's eyes practically glowed as Dave told him about receiving Sarah's antidote and ingesting her blood. "We'll have to run more tests right away."

Dave sighed. "Now? Can't I rest first? I'm glad to

even stand on my own two feet."

"Don't worry, you can sleep during most of them." Ian ushered him into a hospital room. "Lie down and sleep if you like, and I'll hook you up to our monitors and take some blood."

He's more interested in my blood than she was. He chuckled wryly. Since exhaustion overcame him, he didn't argue. Instead, he stretched on the bed and closed his eyes. Her reassuring smile flashed in his mind as he drifted off to sleep.

Once again, he woke to the beeping of hospital monitors. This time, his head was clear and his body well rested. Judging by the sun's position, he'd slept through the rest of the night and most of the day.

Since his mouth felt dry, he appreciated the bottle of water next to his bed. When the liquid washed the remaining taste of blood from his mouth, a realization hit him. Sarah had actually cured him. He put the bottle down and rubbed his eyes. She was his enemy, wasn't she? At least he'd treated her as such. So why had she saved his life?

His grumbling stomach reminded him he hadn't eaten solid food for almost two days. He removed the monitor cables measuring his vitals from his body and got up. After freshening up in the room's built-in bathroom, he headed to the community kitchen to prepare a turkey sandwich.

His mouth watered as he planted himself on a chair with his food in hand.

"Uncle Dave!" Lily came running the moment he bit into his sandwich.

He swallowed quickly. "Hey there, how are you? Hope I didn't scare you yesterday."

"Didn't scare us." She twirled her left pigtail. "But you worried us. A lot."

"Sorry…I promise I'm fine now." He took another bite.

"So…what happened? Did Aaron help you with the poison?"

"Aaron?" He scratched his cheek. His memories of the previous night were fuzzy. "Oh right, you got him for me, didn't you? Thank you. He brought me to the one who cured me."

"Who cured you?"

He leaned in close and lowered his voice. "A vampire."

Lily gaped at him.

"It's our little secret, yeah?" he added, knowing full well she'd tell Anthony and Tim. They'd pester him about the details later.

"Okay." A wide grin spread across her face. "So, will you read to us again tonight?"

"Sure. But let me take care of a few other things before."

Chapter 8

Carrying two full shopping bags, Dave visited Sarah in her cell around dusk.

She sat up straight, sniffed the air, and the cutest smile spread across her lips. "You're fine!"

A warm feeling built in his chest. "Yes, all thanks to you."

When he looked at the petite woman on the other side of the bars, he didn't see a monster any longer. *She didn't have to save me, and yet she did. She really is nothing like other vampires.*

"What do you need?" Her sky-blue eyes sparkled when she met his gaze, and his heartbeat quickened.

Given what she was, he couldn't let her leave, but he could ensure she didn't live like an animal. "I wanted to give something to you. How would you like to make yourself more comfortable down here?"

She frowned. "What do you mean?"

Her eyes bulged when he pulled a pillow and a blanket out of the shopping bags.

"I didn't cure you to get anything in return. Seeing you alive and well is all I hoped for."

He raised an eyebrow, and his lips quirked. "Oh, so you don't want them?"

She nibbled on her lower lip, and a blush colored her cheeks red. "I didn't say that."

"Good, because I bought them just for you." He

chuckled and opened her cell door with a key, breaking the rule of never entering a vampire's cell without at least one more hunter present. "I'm coming in."

He put the pillow on her bed and gave her the blanket. She wrapped herself up in it and hummed happily. "Thank you."

"You're welcome. Is there anything else you'd like?"

"Well...blood." She licked her lips, and his heart skipped a beat. Had he misjudged her? When he took a step back, she added, "I'm talking about bagged blood, obviously."

"Of course. Good thing I already picked up a bag on the way here." He relaxed, pulled it from his coat pocket, and handed it to her. "Do you actually enjoy drinking this kind of blood?"

She nodded, bit into the bag, and emptied the contents. Strangely, the sight didn't disgust him anymore.

"Despite its insipid taste, I prefer drinking from a bag because it minimizes the risk of me hurting anyone."

"Huh. Apart from necessities like blood, is there anything else you'd enjoy?"

She stared at him blankly. "I don't know."

He raked a hand through his hair. "How about reading? I'm sure you're bored, and diving into a book is a great way to pass the time."

She shrugged. "Blood is the only thing my body craves."

Why did she care so little about her well-being? He sighed. "I'll see if I can come up with something, anyway. I've got some errands to run, but I'll be back tomorrow night. And Dr. Crowley intends to speak with you about the effects of vampire blood sometime this week as well."

****

When the door cracked open in the early afternoon, Sarah expected to see Dave or Dr. Crowley. Yet no one descended the stairs.

Faint voices whispered upstairs. Children? They debated whether to enter the dungeon. Eventually, they decided against it.

Their small footsteps veered away from the door, only to return an hour later. This time, they opened it all the way. A little boy, no more than eight years old, sneaked down to glance at her before hurrying back up. Hushed voices echoed through the corridor. Then, three kids padded to her cell.

Apart from the boy, there was a girl around the same age with brown pigtails, wearing a beautiful red dress, and another much younger boy.

Sarah smiled. "Hello there."

The girl shrieked.

"Let's go," the older boy said, and the three ran outside.

What are they up to? The dungeon was no place for kids to play. She sighed.

****

Once the world quieted down around her and night fell, Dave visited again, causing happy butterflies to flutter through her belly.

He handed her a bag of blood, a flashlight, and a selection of novels. "I picked up some of my favorite classics from the library. Hopefully, there's something you enjoy."

Tilting her head, she inspected the items. "I've never

read for pleasure before."

"What do you do for pleasure, then?"

"Nothing, really. I haven't had the luxury of indulging in anything fun for a long time." She bit her lip.

He frowned. "You must have a hobby or something? How did you spend your time growing up?"

"As a child, I loved music, so my parents signed me up for ballet lessons. This part of my childhood feels like a different world now. One I left behind on my seventh birthday. I didn't grow up like other humans. Learning, fighting, eating, and sleeping took up all of our time. We weren't allowed to pursue any hobbies."

"We?"

The image of three girls flashed before her eyes, but she shook it from her head. "Never mind. I'll give the books a try."

After staring at her for a moment, he sighed. "Okay."

****

When the three kids returned the next day, Sarah stayed quiet and watched their approach with an amused expression.

"Hello," the girl said without meeting Sarah's eyes. Her cheeks turned rosy.

"Hey," she replied. "What are you doing here?"

The girl glanced at her two companions—the older boy with short blond hair, wearing a blue-and-green-striped shirt and a pair of jeans, and the younger boy in a yellow sweatshirt with a large elephant print, who was hiding halfway behind the older one. Since the two boys didn't react, the girl answered, "We heard about a vampire who saved Uncle Dave."

"Uncle Dave?" she asked. "Are you related?"

The bigger boy shook his head. "Not really. But we're all a big family here!"

"Really? How nice." She smiled at him. "And why did you want to see me?"

"Did you save Uncle Dave?" the young boy asked with gigantic eyes.

She nodded. "I guess I did."

"Thank you!" the three kids said in unison.

"Why are you thanking me?"

"We were really worried about Uncle Dave. He often plays with us and reads stories to us. But when he was sick from the poison, he collapsed in our room," the older boy explained.

"That must have been terrifying. I'm glad I could help."

"What's your name?" the girl asked.

"I'm Sarah. Who are you?"

"Lily."

"I'm Tim, and the boy behind me is Anthony," the older boy said.

Anthony hid his face behind his hands, glancing through his fingers.

"Nice to meet you three." Sarah tilted her head. "Is it okay for you to be down here?"

The kids exchanged an uneasy glance.

Tim crossed his arms in front of his body. "We can go wherever we want."

"Really?" She narrowed her eyes, and the kids nodded. "Just to make sure, I'll ask Dave the next time I see him."

"Please don't," Lily blurted out.

She chuckled. "So, it's not okay for you to be here

after all?"

"Dave worries too much about us," Tim said.

"He's right to worry. It's dangerous for kids like you to go down into the dungeon. The cells are full of wicked monsters."

"You're not dangerous, are you?" Anthony asked in a faint voice.

She sighed. "All vampires are dangerous. I'm no exception."

"You don't look dangerous," Lily said.

Sarah hissed, showing her fangs. "How about now?"

Lily yelped, and Anthony cowered behind Tim, who stood his ground despite trembling slightly.

For their safety, it would be better if they feared her and stayed away.

"If you leave now and don't come back, I won't tell Dave about your visit," she proposed.

They nodded and dashed away.

Chapter 9

"Are you even listening?" Emily tapped her fingers on the kitchen table, pulling Dave from his thoughts.

He blinked at his colleagues. Aaron was watching him with a raised eyebrow, and Charles was still eating his bagel.

He put his coffee down and turned his attention to Emily. "Sorry...What were you saying?"

She sighed with exaggeration. "Although we spent the last three nights looking for the vampire who attacked you, we didn't find a trace of him."

"I'm not surprised. He's probably long gone. Considering his messy feeding habits, I'm sure we'll stumble upon him again, eventually."

"Why aren't you more upset?" she asked. "You almost died."

Almost, yes. So right now, he was more interested in the vampire who'd ensured he didn't die. But they wouldn't understand. He didn't even understand why he couldn't get her out of his head, why she'd saved him, or why his heart jounced whenever she was close. "There's no use in getting upset about things we can't change. Instead, we should focus on cases where we can make a difference."

Emily pouted.

"I agree," Aaron said. "With every bloodsucker we kill, we make the world a better place. So, where are we off to next?"

He placed a case file on the table. "Portland. You can take charge, Aaron, because I'll sit this one out."

Aaron eyeballed him. "Why? You look fine to me."

"I don't think I'm ready for battle yet." He avoided Aaron's gaze. "Besides, there's some stuff I need to do."

"Fine. Just make sure you're in top form for our next mission." Aaron grabbed the file and thumbed through it before handing it to Charles. "It's a long drive to Portland. We'll leave right away and study the details on the way."

Once his teammates left, he downed the last of his coffee and headed for the lab.

Ian was experimenting with several liquids—most of them looked a lot like blood—in test tubes. He startled when Dave let the lab door fall shut with a thud. A drop of a clear liquid fell from a pipette into one of the test tubes, and the thick, red fluid within hissed and steamed at the contact. "Damn it," he mumbled before looking up. "Hey, Dave."

"Sorry, I didn't mean to mess up your experiment."

"Don't worry about it." He picked up the test tube and held it to the light. "What can I help you with?"

"When you examined Sarah, you extracted some of her DNA as well, didn't you?"

"Yes, it's standard procedure to determine the vampire's origins and estimate their true age." Ian looked at him with a frown. "Why do you ask?"

He averted his gaze. "Can you give me the results? I'd like to verify some things she told me."

Ian narrowed his eyes. "Don't you think you're getting a little obsessed with her?"

He ran his fingers through his hair. "She saved my

life. I wish to understand why."

After studying him for a moment, Ian nodded. "Her DNA matches with the sample of a seven-year-old from an abduction case near Portland over eleven years ago. I believe her full name is Sarah McAllister."

His eyes widened. "Why would vampires kidnap a child?"

"Beats me. She wasn't the only victim, though. I've added a copy of the article to her file, so you can check it out."

"Thanks." He picked up the file for "Test Subject 057." Somewhere in the back, the black-and-white picture of a little girl smiling with a gap between her teeth greeted him. The adjoining text froze the blood in his veins.

Police found the bodies of John and Cassidy McAllister and their five-year-old son Cody in their home yesterday. Their daughter Sarah, who turned seven on Tuesday, is still missing. The family's oldest son was away on a class trip and is now in the care of relatives.

Based on the cake and decorations, the McAllisters were preparing to celebrate their daughter's birthday when the unknown offenders forced their way into the family's home. They beheaded the parents and prepped their bodies at the kitchen table. The young boy died from loss of blood from a wound on his neck.

This is the third in a series of gruesome murder-kidnappings around Portland in the last four months. So far, the police have no suspects and no clues regarding the whereabouts of the missing girls.

****

"I thought you shouldn't be down here," Sarah said when Lily, Tim, and Anthony visited her again two days later. *So much for scaring them away…*

"Tell us a story," Lily said.

"Afterward, we'll go back upstairs," Tim promised.

Anthony simply nodded.

"A story, huh?" She scratched her chin. "About what?"

"Anything. Maybe a fairy tale?" Lily proposed.

"Well, I can't say no to a fairy tale." A smile spread across her face. "Do you know the one about a girl in a red hood—"

"Little Red Riding Hood?" Anthony said. "We already know that one."

"Can you tell us a…vampire…fairy tale?" Tim asked breathlessly.

"A vampire fairy tale?" She chuckled. "Well, I'll give it a try."

"Great!" The kids jumped for joy.

She waited a moment until they settled down in front of her cell, watching her with keen eyes.

"Once there was a little girl, around the same age as Lily. She also had two brothers and lived happily with her family in a roomy house in the suburbs. One day, an evil vampire kidnapped her from her home. He kept the girl prisoner to drink her blood and compelled her to serve him for years. When she was old enough, he turned her into a vampire, forcing her to do his evil bidding for eternity."

Tim gasped. "Poor girl!"

"We need a prince to save her," Anthony said.

"Yet no prince came to her rescue." She grimaced. "All the girl ever wanted was a normal life, but she had no say in the matter. However, the evil vampire had miscalculated. Becoming a vampire made the girl much faster and stronger than before, and she finally got away from her kidnapper."

"Yes!" Lily squealed. "Did she return to her family?"

"No. Being a monster made it impossible for her to live among humans. And she could not forgive the evil vampire for what he'd done. In order to take revenge, she sought hunters to help her defeat the vampire."

"And?" Tim asked. "Did they defeat him?"

Not yet. She grew quiet.

"Tell us!" Anthony said.

They want a happy ending. "Well…it took the little vampire girl a while to gain the hunters' trust. Eventually, they fought the evil vampire together and vanquished him, so he would never hurt another girl again."

"What happened to the little vampire girl afterward?" Lily asked.

"What do you think happened to her?"

"I'm sure she became good friends with the hunters and stayed with them." Lily smiled.

Sarah swallowed. "Well, I hope you're right."

"Thank you for the exciting story," Tim said.

"Don't forget, you promised to leave right after the story," she reminded them.

Reluctantly, they said their goodbyes.

****

Visiting Sarah for a chat and bringing her a nightly bag of blood quickly became part of Dave's routine. Every time she smiled at him, warmth radiated through his body. How did someone who grew up among monsters turn into such a wonderful person? He longed to get to know her better. They mostly talked about inconsequential things, like the books he brought her.

"What did you think about *1984*?" Their fingers touched briefly when she handed her latest read back to him through the bars of her cell.

"I don't understand why humans write about dystopian worlds…As if the world they lived in wasn't bad enough already." She wrinkled her nose.

"Most humans don't know about vampires and other dreadful creatures lurking in the dark."

She considered his words with a faraway look in her eyes. "They're lucky."

"Ignorance might be bliss, but without hunters keeping them safe from the shadows, it could get them killed."

"Keeping all of them safe…That's quite a burden you carry on your shoulders."

"I guess…" He sighed. "Do you ever wonder what your life would be like if you'd never encountered a vampire?"

She shook her head. "As a seven-year-old, I only had unrealistic dreams, like becoming a famous ballet dancer. After they took me, I quickly learned I had no say in my future, so I stopped picturing what it could be like."

"And now?"

"Why wonder about something unattainable? It won't change my fate."

With no aspirations or dreams, what was she living for? If only he could save her from the darkness in her mind. He cleared his throat from the forming lump and changed the topic. "So, what kind of book would you like to read next?"

"Have you got some kind of fairy tale collection?"

"Fairy tales? Why?" He raised his eyebrows.

"I devoured them as a child. Besides, I should brush up on my fairy tales because I've had some visitors lately who love them as much as I did at their age."

"Who are you talking about?"

"I believe their names were Lily, Tim, and Anthony."

His stomach clenched at the mention of the kids' names. What were they doing playing in the dungeon?

She squashed her lips together. "I've told them they shouldn't come down here. They wouldn't listen, though. Sorry."

"It's not your fault." He inhaled deeply. "They're sweet kids, but always up to no good. I'll talk to them."

"Don't their parents pay attention to where they're going?"

"They're orphans—their parents were hunters who died on the job. Now, the hunter community raises them."

"They told me you're like a big family."

"We are." He smiled, thinking about them. "This compound comprises over two hundred people. Not all of them actively hunt vampires. Some help with other daily tasks, administrative work, or research. We've also got families with small kids and retired people. They're all part of our community, and we take care of each other."

She smiled wistfully. "Sounds nice."

"It's one of the pleasant aspects of this life. We face so many horrors, and we've lost so much…But our community helps us persevere."

"I'm sorry," she whispered.

"Don't be. It's not your fault. We chose this life

ourselves."

"I bet it wasn't much of a choice."

"Maybe not." He stared at the wall, considering his words. "This life is the only one I know, and I try to make the best of it, like every one of us. While I hate the violence, as long as there are no better options, I'll keep fighting to protect everyone."

Chapter 10

A few days later, Sarah was reading the fairy tale of *Hansel and Gretel* when an electric tingling in the air sent chills down her body. She recognized the sensation as the aura of a vampire informing others of his presence. But what was a vampire with such a potent energy doing at the compound? The hunters wouldn't have been able to capture him unless...

Blood brothers and sisters, listen to my call. I'm at the hunters' base, broadcasting my location to all of you. Follow my aura and join me in the fight to obliterate these pesky humans. Gather nearby, and when the clock strikes midnight, ambush them as an army. They won't know what hit them.

The foreign voice echoing in her head confirmed her suspicion, and her stomach rolled. The vampire emanated power, possessed telepathic abilities, and was out for the hunters' blood.

Based on the fatigue pulling on her consciousness, the sun was already up, so they had less than eighteen hours until the attack. And she had no way to warn the hunters from her cell. Should she simply wait for Dave's next visit? Or should she make a scene to draw their attention? Causing trouble would not incite them to heed her warnings.

She chewed her nails while running through plausible scenarios in her mind. If Dave brought her blood around dusk, would the time suffice for them to prepare to fight back? Could they fend off an army of vampires at all? If not, how could she aid them in their struggle?

Her heart jerked in her chest when the door opened. She perched on the edge of the stone bed as Lily, Tim, and Anthony sneaked down to her cell. Luckily, they rarely listened to what the grown-ups told them.

"Hello," Anthony said with a wide grin.

"Hey," she said. "As far as I remember, you're not supposed to visit me. And yet here you are."

The grin vanished from Anthony's face, and he hid behind Tim.

"Sorry," Tim said sheepishly. "No one's got time to play with us, so we hoped you could tell us another story."

"Not today…" She chewed her lower lip. "There is something I want you to do."

Lily narrowed her eyes. "Why should we do something for you?"

"It's nothing bad, but it's important. In return, I promise to tell you a captivating fairy tale the next time you come to visit."

"Deal." Tim grinned. "So, what do you need?"

"Do you know where Dave is?"

Tim nodded. "Yeah, he's probably in his room, sleeping."

"All right. I need you to go to his room, wake him up, and tell him to come see me as soon as possible."

"Why?" Lily asked.

Sarah's gaze darted to the ground. "Please, just trust me. It's crucial I talk to him."

"Okay." Lily gestured to her two little friends to

follow her, and they scampered upstairs.

Dave arrived at her cell ten minutes later with disheveled hair, wearing a blue tracksuit.

"I assume you didn't ask the kids to wake me for no reason, so what's wrong?" he asked through a yawn.

"An army of vampires will ambush this compound tonight."

"What?" He blinked at her.

"There's a vampire here, calling upon all nearby vampires to storm the compound at midnight."

"What?" he asked again with wide eyes.

She raised an eyebrow. "Do you honestly need me to repeat it again?"

"No." He shook his head. "I just didn't expect this when I woke. How many?"

She closed her eyes and concentrated on the supernatural auras in their vicinity. "So far, about two dozen. I bet more will gather once the sun sets."

"Shit."

"Can you handle several dozen vampires?"

He rubbed his jaw. "I'm not sure. We've got a bit more than a hundred active hunters right now. As long as the ratio is three to one or better, we'll stand a chance."

Assuming they merely faced weak vampires. "I don't like these odds."

"Me neither. What would you suggest?"

"First, get rid of the vampire who's calling them. But be careful when you approach him."

"Why?" He frowned.

"Judging by his aura, he's a few hundred years old, which makes him extremely strong. Truth be told, I don't think you could have caught him unless he wanted you to."

"Are you saying we couldn't handle a powerful vampire?"

She nodded. "No offense, but you can't."

"Some taken. Don't underestimate us. We've been hunting vampires for years."

"Yet you don't know some basic facts about us, like our supernatural abilities or the fluids we inject with our bite."

"You've got a point." He scraped a hand through his hair. "Do you have any other suggestions?"

She hesitated. Should she offer her help fighting them? They would never accept it. "No. Good luck."

"Thank you."

****

After the emergency meeting he'd called, the whole compound was abuzz with hunters preparing for battle and non-combatants moving into the building's lower levels, setting traps, and fortifying doors and windows. Everyone knew the contingency plans, but no one expected they'd ever need to resort to them. The worry and fear etched into most faces almost suffocated Dave, and his stomach roiled.

An ear-splitting crash in the distance made him cringe. Nearby hunters looked around the room, searching for the origin of the noise, before taking off toward the eastern dungeon. He followed them, dragging his footsteps. They held the vampire responsible for the ambush in a cell there. Sarah's words rang in his head— *I don't think you could have caught him unless he wanted you to*—and they chilled him to the bone.

A gaping hole graced the outer wall of the vampire's cell. The bodies of two hunters lay on the ground, surrounded by debris. The monster had ripped their hearts from their chest before they could execute him.

Dizziness overcame him, and his legs gave in. Before he dropped to the ground, someone grabbed him from behind, supporting his weight.

"You okay?" Charles asked.

He drew in a deep breath and steadied himself. "Yes, thank you. The sight...it's..."

"We'll make them pay." Charles studied him. "You're pale. Why don't you lie down for a second or eat something before the fight? We've got a little over two hours till midnight."

"I'll get something later. For now, we need to prepare. How are Aaron and Emily doing?"

"They're discussing last-minute strategies with the others in the community room. We should join them."

"Good idea. But first, I need to take care of something. You go ahead without me." He forced a smile.

"All right. See you soon," Charles said and left.

He scurried to the southern dungeon. On the way, he made a detour to the kitchen to pick up a bag of blood for Sarah and a banana for himself.

"Here." He tossed her the bag without another word of greeting. While she quenched her thirst, he gobbled down the banana. Hopefully, having some food in his stomach would help ease his nerves.

"You don't look so good. What's wrong?" she asked after putting the bag down.

"The vampire you warned us about broke free, killing two hunters."

She grimaced. "I'm sorry."

"I need to know how many vampires are lurking nearby."

"Okay." She closed her eyes. After a moment of concentrating, her hands balled into fists. "You don't really want to know."

"Tell me." He clenched his jaw. "We need to know."

"I count roughly fifty vampires. Possibly more."

He swallowed, and his mind turned blank.

"You have the element of surprise, though. They don't know you know they're coming," she said half-heartedly.

"Based on what I saw in the other dungeon, the element of surprise won't be enough to win."

When he turned to leave, her voice stopped him. "Dave, wait."

"What is it?"

"Do you trust me?" She bit her lip.

Did he? She'd saved his life, so…He nodded slowly.

"Do you trust me enough to let me save you?"

"What do you mean?" He frowned.

"If the vampires are winning, will you let me out of this cell so I can fight for you?"

His eyes widened. Was she hoping to use the situation to her advantage to gain her freedom?

"I'm supposed to trust you to fight on our side against your own kind?" He yearned to trust her, but this was madness. A sigh escaped his lips. "Besides, what difference could a fledgling like you possibly make?"

"Maybe there's more to me than meets the eye." She avoided his gaze.

Had naivety and hope clouded his judgment? His stomach dropped. "Are you implying you're also stronger than you've made us believe?"

She brought her legs up to the stone bed, hugging them to make herself appear smaller. "I'm not sure how strong or weak you think I am. I've made no claims regarding my strength."

"What games are you playing? I don't have time for this." Without sparing her another glance, he ascended the stairs.

"If, at some point, you've got nothing left to lose, please remember my offer. I won't betray you!" she called after him.

Chapter 11

The vampires descended on the compound like a swarm of angry wasps. Since they didn't expect resistance, the first few dropped like flies. Yet their comrades' deaths didn't deter the horde of bloodthirsty beasts.

The hunters fought in teams of twos or threes. Dave fought alongside Charles against an Asian-looking vampire with nunchucks. With his foreign weapon, he kept them at a distance.

Dave met his colleague's eyes and mouthed the word "net." Once Charles nodded, he charged at the vampire. When his sword locked with the nunchucks, a grin spread across his opponent's face.

With a swift move of his arm, the vampire wrapped the chain of his weapon around Dave's sword. Spinning around, he forced Dave to release the hold on his weapon to keep his arm from breaking.

The moment the sword hit the ground, Charles hurled a silver net over the beast's body. Hissing, the vampire drew his hands up to shield his head.

Dave drew a silver dagger from his belt and tackled the vampire. When they hit the ground, he plunged his weapon into the beast's heart, killing him.

His pulse raced, and he took a deep breath. *One down, countless more to go.*

Since the net entangled his sword as well, he folded

it up to retrieve his weapon.

"Look out!" Charles' voice rang in his ears.

He turned around in time to see his team member jumping in front of a rabid vampire with long, black hair, wearing a black leather dress.

She cried out as Charles used his sword to tear a hole into her stomach, but the injury didn't deter her. Ravenously, she lunged at Charles and sank her teeth into his flesh. Groaning, he collapsed with her on top of him.

Once Dave got a hold of his sword, he stormed at them and pierced the vampire's heart from behind. Seconds before she died, she ripped out Charles' throat.

Blood gushed from the hunter's neck, coloring everything around them red. Flashes from his past popped up in the back of Dave's mind, threatening to overwhelm him. His parents' corpses. Their living room, painted in blood. Maya's panicked cry for help.

But Charles needed him, so he pushed his dark memories aside to focus on his colleague and friend.

Frantically, he tried to stop the bleeding with his hands, pressing them against the deep gash. No matter how firmly he pressed, it was no use. The blood kept flowing until all life had oozed out of Charles' body.

"No!" he wailed, and his knees gave in.

All around him, the fight was still raging. Corpses of vampires and hunters littered the battlefield. And the odds were against them. Most hunters fought alone or in pairs against one or two vampires. They defended themselves fiercely, but how long would their will to fight last when the bodies of their comrades surrounded them? *It's over, isn't it? We've lost.*

Sarah's face flashed in front of his eyes. *I really am*

desperate.

With the last of his strength, he forced himself to his feet and staggered inside.

The building's main hall was eerily quiet. Everyone was fighting outside or hiding in the lower levels. No one was around to keep him from releasing her.

He opened the large door to the southern dungeon with his blood-smeared hands and descended the stairs.

She was rocking on the bed, her arms wrapped around her knees. When he stopped in front of her cell, she looked up expectantly.

"I've seen too many hunters die tonight to delude myself any longer. We won't make it." He unlocked the cell door. "I probably won't even live long enough to regret this."

She tilted her head and met his eyes. "There'll be nothing to regret, I promise."

Slowly, he approached her. Since his hands trembled, he needed several tries to remove the manacles from her wrists and the collar from her neck with his tiny key. All the while, she stayed as still as a statue. Was she waiting for the right moment to...do what, exactly?

"All right." He gulped. "Follow me."

****

Sarah stretched her stiff muscles and followed Dave slowly, so as not to frighten him, up the stairs and through the large hall. They left the building through the main entrance.

Outside, she surveyed the battlefield. Around forty vampires fought against almost twice as many hunters. The vampire who'd called for this ambush was among them, effortlessly battling a group of five.

The mouth-watering scent of blood in the air toyed

with her mind. *Why not join the feast?* the beast in her whispered. She silenced it with a roar.

Dave flinched next to her. Even though she'd expected as much, a wave of disappointment rolled over her. He feared her just like any other vampire. Ignoring the heavy feeling in her stomach, her eyes searched the battlefield for her first opponent. She needed to even the odds for the hunters before she faced the leader of the vampire army.

A few meters to her left, two hunters fought a vampire with a saber—her favorite kind of weapon.

She stormed at the vampire, tackled him to the ground, and ripped his heart out of his chest. His two opponents gaped at her.

She wiped her bloody hand on the vampire's clothes, picked up his weapon, and inspected it. When the perfectly balanced blade cut her finger, it burned. *Silver. Isn't it funny how they brought the weapon of their demise?*

A pair of vampires—a female redhead and a male punk with a green mohawk and a machete—were closing in on a single human. Since she didn't like his chances, she sprinted to his aid. With one swift motion, she cut the head off the male vampire. The female cried out in anger and despair.

"Oh, I'm sorry, were the two of you close? Don't worry, I'll send you to the same place as him."

"How dare you, traitor!" With a dagger in each hand, the woman charged at her.

She deflected each strike. With an upward swinging slash, she split the vampire in half, from her core to her head.

The human they'd targeted stared at the scene with

an open mouth. When she turned to him, he took a step back.

"Are you all right?" she asked, and he nodded. "Then help someone else."

Two female hunters panted nearby. They could barely stay on their feet while their opponent, a dark-skinned vampire, smiled triumphantly. When he went for a finishing blow, she stepped in and blocked his sword with her saber.

"What are you doing?" he asked.

Instead of replying, she swung her weapon at him. The vampire barely deflected her first three strikes. With the fourth, she severed his right arm. His hand still clung to his sword as it tumbled to the ground. Her next stab pierced his heart. When she pulled her saber from his chest, he fell to the ground, dead.

In a similar fashion, she brought down fourteen more vampires. Since she reckoned the hunters could take care of their remaining opponents, she turned her attention to the army's leader.

A group of hunters surrounded the fat, bald-headed vampire in leather armor, but he merely toyed with them. Based on the enormous power emanating from him, he could finish them in seconds. And if he realized his pawns were losing, he'd squash the humans without a second thought.

Sarah gulped. She needed to catch his attention without endangering them. After taking a deep breath, she released her dark powers and let them flow over the battlefield. Every vampire in her vicinity turned and looked at her.

Several hunters took advantage of this distraction and pierced their opponents' hearts or cut off their heads, thus reducing the number of vampires to less than twenty.

The vampire leader narrowed his eyes at her. "You're on their side."

She shrugged. "Yes. So what?"

He appeared right in front of her with his sword raised. "I'll kill you for your treason!"

"You can try." She evaded the slash of his weapon with ease.

"Not bad." He looked her up and down. "Guess I'll have to fight seriously."

Although she blocked each blow of his sword, the force he put behind his attacks took a toll on her. Age made him stronger, but it did not make up for his lack of flexibility due to obesity. Could she get the upper hand if she evaded his blade instead of parrying?

When the bald-head swung his weapon at her again, she elegantly swirled out of reach. Every other time, she used her momentum to land a hit on him. They danced like this for minutes, and with each slash, the color of her opponent's face turned into a darker shade of red and his nostrils flared.

With a growl, he let his sword drop and threw himself at her. They toppled to the ground, and he bit into her shoulder, tearing a piece of flesh from her body. She cried out as an excruciating burst of pain shot through her, and blood painted her clothes and her vision red. But she'd dealt with worse. The agony would not last forever, and such a wound would not kill her.

Gritting her teeth, she turned her attention to her opponent. He stood above her, his legs spread wide, his fangs dripping with her blood, laughing at his perceived victory.

She tightened her grip on the saber in her hand. As quick as lightning, she lifted her upper body, spun her arm, and pierced his heart with her weapon.

Wide-eyed, the vampire staggered back, clutching at the blade in his chest. Color blanched from his face, and he sank to his knees. She got to her feet. With one swift move, she withdrew her saber and used it to remove his head.

The wound on her shoulder still throbbed, but the bleeding slackened. She moaned slightly as she took in her surroundings. Only a handful of vampires remained, and each of them was up against four or more hunters. Every hunter who wasn't fighting or taking care of the injured stared at her.

****

Dave could not believe his eyes. How did this petite vampire, who surrendered to them a fortnight ago, defeat a third of the attacking army and their monstrous leader with ease? Her precise and flowing movements mesmerized him as she struck down one vampire after the other, never harming a human. The last battle had wounded her, though, and she staggered in his direction.

The battlefield quieted down. Only her footsteps broke the silence.

All eyes focused on her—and whose eyes wouldn't? This stunning woman had saved them.

Yet the other hunters didn't share his sentiment. Some tightened the grip on their weapon, some took a step or two back as she passed them, and others searched their comrades' faces for hints or gaped at her.

He met her gaze. Was it fear he saw in there? Did they truly scare her, and if so, why didn't she run?

Her eyes never left his as she let her weapon drop to

the ground with a *clang*. Slowly, she kept walking toward him. About three meters from him, she raised her hands in surrender and kneeled down.

A murmur emerged around them. "Why did she fight for us?" "Should we secure her?" "Is this a trap?" "Better kill her while we can."

He balled his fists. If he didn't act fast, they'd turn against their savior. He didn't blame them because he knew the fear and hatred they felt for her kind. But Sarah differed from the monsters they despised.

With a sigh, he took the silver manacles from his belt and stepped forward.

"Sorry," he whispered while cuffing her hands behind her back. *This is wrong. We should celebrate her for saving us.*

"It's all right," she said.

Another hunter approached and handed him a silver net. With a grimace, he wrapped it around her body. She flinched beneath his hands, but she didn't protest.

"Let's get you inside." He wrapped his arms around her waist, helped her to her feet, and steered her toward the main building.

The other hunters backed off, watching them with distrust. To appease them, he brought her back to her cell.

As soon as they were out of sight, he removed the net. The others wouldn't condone an unsecured vampire in their home, though. Reluctantly, he chained her to the wall like before.

Blood had soaked her clothes red.

"Your shoulder is still bleeding. Will you be all right?" he asked.

"As soon as I get fresh blood."

He fetched two bags from the kitchen. His stomach churned when she thanked him for them. Everything about this felt wrong. She shouldn't be the one thanking him. She shouldn't be in a cell. Most of all, she shouldn't be their prisoner. How could he rectify this situation if she surrendered so willingly? If she didn't put her needs first, he'd do it for her. But how?

To begin with, he longed to understand her reasons. Yet this wasn't the time for chats. "I need to check on the situation upstairs. I promise I'll be back soon."

Chapter 12

Sarah bounced her legs while waiting for Dave. Had she lost his trust by saving him? Did he fear her after seeing her true strength? Her throat constricted. How would he handle the truth?

When he finally returned, he carried a bucket full of water in one hand and a pile of towels, clothes, and soap in his other arm. "I thought you'd like to clean yourself up and put on new clothes."

She blinked at the sight, not sure how to respond.

"I know it's not ideal, but it's the best I can do for now." He opened the cell door and placed the items on the bed next to her. "I'll remove the chains and leave you alone for a moment so you can undress and wash yourself."

"Thanks," she mumbled.

With a warm smile, he unlocked the manacles and chain around her neck. "I hope you'll find something you like among these clothes."

Once he left, she removed her stained outfit and washed the blood and dirt off her body with a washcloth. After drying herself, she rummaged through the clothes and decided on a comfy, light blue tracksuit.

"Are you decent?" he asked a few minutes later from upstairs.

"Yes."

"Good." He descended the stairs with another bag of

blood in his hands. "I bet you're still hungry after the blood you lost."

"I'm always hungry."

He tossed the bag to her and leaned back against the wall.

"Are there many casualties?" she asked before sinking her teeth into the bag.

His face darkened. "We lost twenty-two people last night, and around thirty hunters got severely injured. If it wasn't for you, it would have been a lot worse."

He fell silent as she emptied the bag. When she tossed it back to him, he asked, "Why?"

She frowned. "You'll have to ask more precise questions. I promise to answer all of them, though."

"Why did you pretend to be young and weak?"

"I pretended nothing. After all, I am eighteen years old, and I've only been a vampire for a couple of months. I never claimed to be weak. You merely assumed so."

"You didn't correct our assumption."

She chuckled. "You never asked. Besides, I didn't want to scare you."

"Why not? Why surrender and let us put you in a cell? From what I've seen, you could probably break out if you wanted to…"

She pressed her lips tightly as she considered her answer. "Possibly. But I don't know for sure, and I don't intend to find out. I truly aim to help, and I didn't know how else to approach you."

"Approach us?" He tilted his head.

She sighed. "Experience taught me hunters consider every vampire a threat. I was hoping you'd be more open to listening if you had me securely locked somewhere."

"Why do you want to fight your own kind so badly?

What happened to you?" His eyes searched hers.

"Do you really want to know my story?"

He nodded.

She exhaled loudly. "I only remember glimpses of my childhood before everything changed on my seventh birthday. My parents' screams woke me around dawn, and I lumbered to the kitchen to find them hunched on the table. I remember pulling on my mother's sleeve, asking if she was all right. My words died mid-sentence when her head came off, rolling to the floor." Her voice shook as memories assaulted her mind. "A whimpering made me turn around in time to see a vampire burying his fangs into my little brother's throat, draining him. Another vampire grabbed me from behind. I cried out, thinking I'd die."

"But they didn't kill you."

"No, death would have been a mercy. They fed on me without numbing the pain until I blacked out. When I woke, I was in a strange place with two other girls my age."

"Were they kidnapped as well?"

She nodded. "It was just the beginning. A few days later, they kidnapped a fourth girl, saying they'd chosen us to become their soldiers. They forced us to drink vampire blood every day to strengthen our bodies, taught us how to fight, and tortured us so we'd become more resilient to pain. Our lives comprised only eating, sleeping, fighting, learning, and suffering.

"When we turned sixteen, they forced us to face each other in a fight to the death. I had to kill a girl, who I'd considered my sister for nine years." A violent shudder went through her body. "Despite everything I'd suffered, this was the worst moment of my life. I vowed to myself to survive, so I could pay them back one day."

His face blanched. "How awful."

"It didn't get any better afterward. They forced us to train even harder every day. With my goal in mind, I put in even more effort, surpassing the remaining girl. On my eighteenth birthday, they turned me and locked me in a room with her. Unable to control my thirst for blood as a newborn vampire, I drained her."

She sucked in a breath when he sat next to her.

"It's all right," he said in a shaky voice. "It wasn't your fault."

She blinked at him, surprised by the tears running down her cheek.

Hesitantly, he closed the distance between them and pulled her into a hug.

Her heart soared at the contact. When was the last time anyone had touched her in a kind way and comforted her? The muscular arms around her shoulders and the warmth of his body sent a pleasurable tingle through her, warming her from the inside.

Although she still trembled from the memory, she continued with her story.

"My kidnappers were jubilant, thinking they'd created the perfect soldier. While they planned to present me to court as a bodyguard for their royal family, I couldn't stand the idea of serving them any longer. Since I wasn't sure if I could defeat them, I used my new powers to run. The first weeks with no one to guide me were tough. I hurt so many people while struggling to suppress the beast in me." A loud sob escaped her. "Only the thought of taking revenge one day prevented me from simply ending my life to protect others. With time, I figured out how to stay in control. I stumbled upon your team of hunters roughly six months later."

"I'm sorry for what you've been through," he said after a moment of silence. "But I still don't understand what role we play in this. I mean, you saved us from an army of vampires…You could take revenge on your own."

"Maybe. But it's an awfully lonely path. I liked the idea of finding people who share my hatred for vampires. In addition, I may be strong, but I'm not invincible. If I lose, there won't be anyone to protect others from suffering the same fate. Humans have the tendency to pass on their knowledge to the next generation. If I shared my experiences with you, you and your descendants could save even more lives."

"What a vision." His voice was heavy with emotion. "Unfortunately, I don't know how to proceed from here. Many of my colleagues fear you for what you are."

"They are right to be scared. I am a monster, after all."

"No, you're not." He grabbed her shoulders, turning her upper body, so she had to look at him. "You're nothing like the vampires who tortured you. I don't think it's fair you're locked up in here after everything you've done for us."

A small smile played on her lips. "Thank you, but I really don't mind. Besides, I can't always restrain my thirst for blood. I don't want to hurt anyone accidentally ever again. Being locked up is the safest option."

He sighed. "It's not my decision, anyway. We've got a meeting at dusk to discuss the aftermath of the attack and…you. Is there anything you'd like me to tell the council members on your behalf?"

"Tell them I'm on your side and willing to help you

in any way possible."

"Do you have anything specific in mind?"

"I could help with the training of your recruits to make them more effective against vampires. Getting actual fighting experience before going into the field might tip the scales in your favor."

"Unless you completely demotivate them." He chuckled.

"I don't need to use my full power to train them. And if they think they stand a chance against me, I'm sure your comrades will be less worried. They never need to know the truth."

He raised an eyebrow. "So, you want me to deceive my colleagues?"

She opened her mouth, struggling for an answer.

"The proposition would appall me if I didn't trust your intentions. But I do, and I agree it's better if they don't know your true strength."

"Well, I'm glad you do." She smiled sheepishly.

"Anyway, it's almost noon, and my body requires sleep before the meeting." His eyes fell to the floor. "I'm afraid I'll have to chain you back up."

"It's okay."

"No, it isn't." He still put the manacles around her wrists.

She shrugged. "I'll gladly wear these if they make the humans living here feel better about my presence."

****

"What do we know about her?" the chairman, a middle-aged man in a gray suit, with an impeccable haircut and shave, asked at the council meeting. He leaned back on his office chair at the head of the massive oval glass table, his arms crossed.

Dave got to his feet and waited until all eyes settled on him. "Like many of us, she suffered at the hands of vampires. Thanks to Ian's DNA analysis, we identified her origins. Her name is Sarah McAllister, and according to old news reports, vampires killed her family and abducted her when she was only seven years old. After torturing her for years, they turned her against her will." The faces of his colleagues softened. Most of them could relate. "Now, she longs for revenge against her tormentors. Those of you who fought last night witnessed her strength."

Some hunters nodded. Others wrinkled their brows.

"Her strength worries me," Ralph, one of the oldest active hunters and Dave's former mentor, said.

"I understand your concern. But let's face it. We wouldn't have survived the night without her. She brought down our enemies while harming none of us. Instead of escaping after our victory—her victory—she surrendered. We should take advantage of her willingness to help."

The members of the council whispered among themselves. The chairman shushed them. "How would you propose to take advantage of her?"

"She's already given Ian valuable information for his studies and will continue to do so. In addition, she's an excellent fighter. So, she could teach us a thing or two and offer hunting practice for our young recruits. With her as an opponent, we can simulate realistic fights without endangering our members."

"Without endangering them?" Ralph asked. "Even if she plays nice now, how do we ensure she won't turn on us and harm or kill anyone during practice?"

Dave glanced at Ian. "I'm sure our science

department can invent some kind of tool to control her."

"Sure." Ian beamed at him. "I've been working on a new gadget."

Really? After what he'd seen, he doubted anything could control her. But if it soothed their worries, he'd take it. "Perfect. Any other concerns?"

Ralph narrowed his eyes, but he did not comment.

"Will you take responsibility for this project?" the chairman asked.

He nodded. "I'm convinced we can benefit from Sarah, so I'm willing to take full responsibility and supervise all training. I'll resign as team lead to put all my time into this. After the losses we suffered last night, we need to restructure our teams, anyway."

"All right," the chairman said. "Let's vote then. Who's in favor of Dave's plan?"

****

Dave beamed at Sarah when he brought her a bag of blood at the end of the night. His upbeat expression eased the knot in her gut.

"I hope your mood is a good sign? How was the meeting?"

He smirked. "I *should* worry about our leaders' complete ignorance and overly optimistic evaluation regarding our abilities to control a powerful vampire like you. But since their ruling was in our favor, I'll simply say it went smoothly."

"What exactly does that mean?"

"Among other things, they agreed to the training. Dr. Crowley's team is still working on a few security measures. We can start once they're done."

"Great!" Her chest lightened at his news. "But what do you mean by 'among other things'?"

"You'll see." He grinned. "I already know the perfect group for our first training."

Chapter 13

Two and a half days later, Sarah had three surprise visitors.

"We heard you saved us from the vampire army," Anthony said.

She nodded. "Did Dave tell you about it?"

"Yes. He also told us you hate vampires because they took away your family and hurt you," Lily said.

"So," Tim said, "we were wondering…The story you told us about the poor girl who got kidnapped by a vampire…was it about you?"

She gasped in a lungful of air. These kids were more perceptive than she'd given them credit for. "Who knows?"

The three kids looked at each other.

"We want to help you defeat the evil vampire," Lily said decidedly. "And we'll be your friends."

She stifled a laugh at their cute offer. "I think you should grow up first before fighting the evil vampire."

"Then we'll grow up really quickly, so you don't have to be afraid of him anymore," Anthony said.

"Thank you, but he doesn't scare me any longer." Warmth spread in her chest. They reminded her of what she was fighting for. She'd bring down every vampire herself to ensure these kids lived carefree lives. "Please take all the time you need to grow up. Enjoy being a child. Seeing you happy makes me happy as well."

The kids whispered among themselves.

"All right," Tim said. "But we'll still be your friends."

****

"No army to lead me through the building?" Sarah joked when Dave came the next night to pick her up for the first training session.

He raised an eyebrow. "I can get one if necessary."

Smiling, she shook her head. She loved spending time alone with him.

"Besides, I've got this little invention from Dr. Crowley here." He held up a silver neck ring. It was slimmer than her collar and finely engraved with a delicate braid pattern, almost like a necklace.

"It's pretty, but I doubt it's any more effective than the other one."

When he approached, she caught a whiff of his rich, fruity scent. Her pulse sped up and her stomach fluttered, even though merely a few hours had passed since her last meal. Why did her body react so strongly to his proximity? She held her breath while he replaced the silver collar around her neck with the new item. Her skin prickled where his fingers brushed against her.

"Oh, but it is." His voice brought her focus back to the gadget. His fingers still lingered at the nape of her neck, sending pleasant shivers down her body. "To ensure our safety during training while giving you full mobility, we can control this collar remotely and use it to inject you with a high dosage of silver nitrate if you misbehave."

"Clever."

"Unfortunately, we still need a few more safety measures while walking through the building." With an apologetic smile, he fastened the familiar helmet on her head and connected a short chain to the manacles around her wrists.

Taking her hand in his, he led her to the garden and from there to a spacious gym building, which comprised a playing field, surrounded by benches on three sides, and a separate area for sports equipment. Bars blocked the gym's windows. Three young hunters in sportswear—a girl with chin-length, black hair, a brown-haired boy, and a tall, blond one with a dragon tattoo on his right arm—were waiting in the middle of the field, whispering to each other with excitement.

Once he removed the manacles and helmet, she stretched her arms and legs. Her muscles longed for some exercise.

"Are you ready?" he asked.

She gestured toward the youths. "Whenever they are."

He turned toward them. "All right, here's your chance to prove you know what you're doing when facing a vampire. Your goal is to defeat and secure her." He parked himself on a bench. "I'll watch the fight from here."

"That's gonna be a piece of cake. After all, she's unarmed." The blond boy gloated.

She burst out laughing. She'd said the same to Dave when they first met. But he'd known the truth…

"Teach them a lesson." Dave smirked.

"You think I'm unarmed?" In the blink of an eye, she appeared right behind the boy.

"Think again, because I've got all I need to suck the life right out of you," she whispered into his ear.

"What the hell!" The anger in his voice didn't hide

his fear as he turned to face her.

"Lesson One: A vampire is always armed. She's got her supernatural speed, her strength, and her fangs," Dave chided them from the bench.

"We know," the girl said through clenched teeth.

"Well then, come at me," Sarah said. "I'll let you have the first shot…if you can hit me at all."

The boys drew their weapons and charged at her while the girl retreated several steps and pulled out a handgun.

As soon as she evaded the slash of the blond boy's sword, the brown-haired one attacked her with two daggers. Their teamwork was exemplary, but they moved too slowly.

The girl's gun was an ill-conceived choice, though. Bringing a gun to a sword fight rarely helped when facing a vampire. It lost its merits when the target was caught in close combat with an ally.

After a few minutes of chasing after her, the boys panted heavily.

"You'll never bring me down with just the two of you," she said.

"Don't forget about me!" the girl shouted and pulled the trigger.

Shit. Within an instant, Sarah realized the bullet would hit the blond boy if she avoided getting shot. She intercepted it with her shoulder.

"Are you fucking stupid?" she snarled as the silver sent waves of pain through her body.

The girl grinned widely. "I hit her!"

"Enough!" Dave rose and bellowed through the gym. "You didn't hit her. Sarah let herself get hit. Why? Because the bullet would have hit Ethan. Never shoot when your target is standing this close to your colleague."

The girl's grin froze.

The blond boy, Ethan, stared at her with wide eyes. "You could have killed me."

"Yes, she could have." Dave glared at the girl. "In an actual fight, the vampire wouldn't take the bullet for you. She'd avoid it with no effort and laugh at your stupidity for killing your comrade. So don't tell me you're ready for the field when you're still making rookie mistakes. Today's training is over. Leave."

As soon as the three left the gym, he turned to Sarah. "Are you okay?"

She crouched on the ground, clutching her shoulder while gritting her teeth. "If you help me remove the bullet, I will be. I'd have thought twice about taking the hit if I'd known they were using actual silver bullets."

"I don't think you would have." His expression softened. "Thank you for not hesitating to take a bullet for these idiots."

"The boys weren't bad, but the girl should have chosen another weapon." She squeezed her eyes shut while he removed the bullet. After several excruciating seconds, the pain subsided.

"They decided on a strategy together. The boys weren't smart enough to realize their backup endangered them. Hunting is not only about fighting skills. Tactics and experience matter as well. If they don't know what they're doing, they won't survive. Hopefully, they learned a lesson tonight."

"I'm sure they did." She forced a smile and met his gaze. "It's just a pity the session ended so quickly. I enjoyed the exercise."

"Despite the bullet?" He frowned. "Take some time to recover first. We can have another one later."

After securing her with the manacles and helmet, he led her outside, through the garden, and back into the main building. He didn't head for the dungeon.

"Aren't we going to my cell?"

"Nope." He chuckled.

She shrugged and followed him without another comment. At least she got to walk a bit more before returning to the narrow cell.

They took a few more turns and ascended a circular stairwell before stopping in front of a white sliding door. When he entered a code on a display on the wall, it opened and revealed a small bedroom hidden behind a transparent glass door with a hatch.

They entered the one square meter space between the two doors. He closed the white one by pressing a button on another display. Using an electronic key card, he opened the glass door. "After you."

Once they were inside, he closed the door, removed her helmet and manacles, and smiled. "Welcome to your new home."

She tilted her head to the side and squashed her eyebrows together. "New home? What?"

"If you're staying and helping us, we can't let you rot in a cell, can we? Together with Ian and his team, I prepared this apartment for you. It's got all the basics: a bed, a wardrobe with a few changes of clothes, and an adjacent bathroom with a shower." He gestured toward the items while she gaped at him. "Since the combination of the collar around your neck, the enforced walls, the silver bars in front of the window, and the two-door system meets our security requirements, you may move freely in here."

Her own room? She blinked. "But why? I'm still a vampire—your enemy."

He rolled his eyes. "Yet you saved us, so this is the least we can do. How could we call ourselves human if we kept you locked in a dark cell?"

Tears built in her eyes. "Thank you."

"No, thank *you*. For everything." His eyes shone as he held her gaze. "I'll give you some time to settle in. Make yourself comfortable, maybe take a shower or something? I'll bring you a bag of blood when I return."

Once he left, she inspected the room more closely. A simple white bed stood to her right. On the opposite side, there was a white wardrobe with two doors. A window on the far wall offered a view of the beautiful garden. She didn't mind the silver bars in front of it, and she appreciated the blinds to shut out the sun during the day.

Near the window, a vase with a single red tulip decorated a wooden table with two chairs. A selection of books lay on a shelf and waited for her to read them.

The tiny adjacent bathroom contained a shower, a toilet, a sink, a mirror, and a towel rail with two towels. A shelf with shampoo, soap, and a brush made her long for a shower. Vampires didn't have the same hygiene requirements as humans, but considering she'd lived in a cell for almost three weeks, freshening up sounded heavenly.

First, she checked out the wardrobe to find socks, underwear, a couple of pants, shirts in various colors, a pair of white sports shoes, and a jacket. She picked an outfit and went for a shower.

The warm water caressed her skin and loosened her

stiff muscles. The bullet wound on her shoulder prickled, but it had mostly healed. Fresh blood would erase any remaining evidence of her injury without leaving scars. The shampoo smelled like chocolate and coconut, reminding her of tastes long forgotten as she massaged her scalp.

After getting dressed and drying her hair with a hair dryer, she relaxed on the bed, wondering if she was dreaming.

Chapter 14

When Dave hastened up the stairwell in the early morning hours, Emily waited on the upper floor. With her arms folded firmly in front of her body, she blocked his way.

Wrinkling her nose, she eyed the bag of blood he carried. "So, Aaron was telling the truth—you actually moved the bloodsucker up to our floor."

"Sarah fought for us. Why shouldn't she get a room like us?"

"Because she's a fucking monster." Emily pursed her lips. "Don't tell me you like her."

With everything that had happened the past three weeks, he hadn't had time to process his emotions. Sarah had grown on him. Occupied his mind. Made his heart race.

Truth be told, he did more than just like her. But admitting his feelings was dangerous, especially since he didn't know how she felt. With her past, she surely had no experience with men. How could he broach the subject without putting her in a bad spot and messing up their alliance? And even if she reciprocated his feelings, could a relationship between a human and a vampire even work?

A heavy sigh escaped him. "We'd be dead without her. And I…care about her."

"Do you even hear what you're saying?"

"Yes. Do you?" He narrowed his eyes at Emily. Despite everything, he knew her well enough to recognize the fear in her accusations. Vampires had killed her little sister while forcing her to watch.

She muttered something under her breath.

He inhaled deeply. Words wouldn't convince her, only time might. There was no use arguing. "Since her room is fully secure, there's nothing for you to worry about. Everything else is none of your business. And she's waiting for me right now, so let's talk later."

"Unbelievable," Emily scoffed. "The bitch got you wrapped around her finger."

Ignoring her comment, he pushed past her.

After entering through the two security doors, he tossed the bag to Sarah and plopped down on a chair. "How do you like your new apartment?"

"I love it!" She beamed at him like a child on Christmas morning. Her infectious smile erased the memory of the unpleasant encounter with Emily.

"You're a lot more enthusiastic than I expected." He chuckled.

"I haven't had a room like this since…" Her voice trailed off. "Is it really okay for me to stay here?"

"Of course. It's only a room."

"Maybe to you. Growing up, I shared an unfurnished room with three other girls. So, this means a lot. Thank you."

"No need to thank me. You might be a vampire, but in my eyes, you're no different from us. You deserve your own room, like everyone else." He lowered his head. "Unfortunately, not everyone agrees, which is why we had to install some security measures."

"Do you feel safe with me?"

"Yes," he answered without hesitation.

She grimaced. "You should reconsider. Right now, I'm in control of the beast in me. But it might overwhelm me at some point. So, your security measures are appropriate."

Why does she keep building walls between us? "Give yourself some credit. I believe in you. What you are doesn't define you, you know?"

She shrugged. "Maybe it doesn't. Maybe it does. I won't risk hurting you. Anyway, did you talk to the three young hunters?"

A change of topic, huh? "Yes, I did. The fight opened their eyes to the dangers of hunting. They almost considered giving it up altogether, but I assured them they only needed more thorough training and better tactics. All things considered, the session had the desired effect."

"I'm glad." A smile returned to her lips.

"Since we're on the topic, could you train with me as well? I want to see your true strength and learn how to go up against powerful vampires like you." *And spend more time with you.*

"Like me?" She drew her eyebrows up. "That's quite ambitious. Humans can't overcome certain barriers...but with the right training, you might surpass an average vampire."

****

After a good day's rest, Dave brought Sarah to the gym again. Like before, he removed the helmet she wore during the transport. He didn't touch the manacles on her wrists, though.

"You can break free from these cuffs yourself, can't you?" he asked.

She bit her lip. "Theoretically."

"Show me."

"Are you sure?" She searched his eyes. "Knowing I might and seeing me break free are two different things. I don't want to freak you out."

"You won't. Please help me understand what you—and other powerful vampires—are capable of." He tightened his fists.

She nodded and closed her eyes.

After a moment, the air sparked with electricity—or did he imagine the sensation?

With a jerk of her arms, she broke the silver chain connecting the cuffs.

When he gasped and retreated half a step, her shoulders slumped slightly. "I knew my powers would scare you."

"No." Shaking his head, he took two steps toward her and put his left hand reassuringly on her shoulder. Making her feel rejected was the last thing he wanted. "You surprised me, is all. Please, show me more!"

"Okay then." She swallowed and backed away. "Come at me and try to land a hit."

He drew his sword. "Just one?"

"One will be hard enough, trust me." She disappeared, only to reappear on the opposite side of the hall with a grin. "I'll give you ten minutes before I go on the offensive."

"All right." He stormed at her.

Every time he approached, she glided out of reach. Whenever he thought he'd cornered her, she vanished. How did she move so incredibly fast? After a while, he bent over, panting.

"If you can't get close, you'll never touch me."

"Well, you're just running away. Looks like you're afraid to face me," he taunted her.

She laughed. "I'm not, and I'll happily prove it to you in—" She glanced at the clock on the gym wall. "—three...two...one...now. Your time is up."

He swallowed and tightened the grip on his sword. "Well then, turn your words into actions because I'm not running either."

"As you wish." She flew at him. With the force of her speed, she pushed him back against the wall. Faster than he could react, she seized his arms with hers and pressed her delicate body against his to keep him from fighting back.

Her soft breasts rubbed against his chest as he struggled against her, and the scent of chocolate and coconut assaulted his senses. She tempted him in more ways than one, and his hands ached to break free and explore her body. A flush of warmth spread through him as he imagined turning their training session into a make-out one. Since this was neither the time nor the place for such thoughts, he shook his head to clear it.

When his jeans tightened, he knew he'd lost the battle—against his arousal. He stilled, hoping she didn't notice the bulge in his pants.

Her eyes focused on his neck, and her fangs protruded from her mouth. Was she fighting a battle against herself as well?

"Are you okay?" he asked, hoping his husky voice didn't betray him.

She winced, released him, and jumped back a few feet. "Sorry. My longing for blood sometimes takes over, especially when I'm close to a human. That's why it's best to keep your distance."

His heart rocketed in his chest, and his left hand wandered to his neck as he pictured her soft lips on his skin. What would it feel like if he offered her his blood? He shook the image from his mind. She clearly wouldn't let it get that far.

"Don't worry, I'm in control now." She cast her eyes downward.

"It's all right," he said. "Thank you for the demonstration. I still got a lot to learn."

And the first thing on his curriculum was how to help her embrace herself and everything life offered without worrying about losing control. Until then, acting on his desires would lead to disaster for too many reasons.

****

When Dave visited her the next night, he carried a mysterious black case in his hand. Did it contain a weapon?

"What is this?" she asked.

With a smile, he set the case on the table, opened it, and revealed a guitar. "You told me about your passion for music as a child. So, I was wondering if you'd like to listen to me play? I must warn you, though, I haven't touched an instrument in years."

She gaped at him. "I…Um…Why?"

He shrugged. "I just felt like it."

Sitting down next to her on the bed, he started playing. The slow and soulful melody tugged at her heart, and the words he sang about life being good and worth saving touched something deep inside of her. A single tear rolled down her cheek.

"Beautiful," she whispered once he finished.

"It's one of my favorite songs. A reminder of the

things life can offer, even when you're at your lowest. It helped me get through a lot of shit."

"Thank you for sharing it with me."

"You're very welcome." The warmth of his eyes caused her heart to flutter. "Would you like me to play more?"

She nibbled on her lip. "If you don't mind."

"Not at all. It would be my pleasure."

After several inspiring songs, he packed up his instrument. "Unfortunately, I don't remember any other pieces. I'll play again for you once I've practiced some more."

"Yes, please." She smiled. "Do you still want to train with me tonight?"

"Definitely. Give me a moment to return my guitar before we head to the gym. My room is down the hall, so I'll be right back."

Strangely, a warm, fuzzy feeling spread in her belly as she thought about his proximity. Even when they slept, he was never far from her.

****

Determined to help Dave push his limits, Sarah spent almost every night training with him at the gym. In between their sessions, she also fought with the young recruits and some of the more experienced hunters who sought a challenge. Yet he was the only one to whom she revealed her true strength.

When she wasn't training, she relaxed in her apartment. He even installed a small TV in her room. Since she hadn't watched TV in years, all the different stories, places, and impressions fascinated her. The human take on her kind confounded her, though. Who'd believe in vampires going to high school and falling in love with one of the other students? While she yearned for peaceful coexistence as well, the monsters she knew wouldn't integrate into human society.

Chapter 15

"Why so glum?" Sarah asked Dave after their latest training session. The warm glow in his eyes and his carefree smile usually set her heart racing. Tonight, he'd lost his shine. In addition, his movements had been extremely sloppy, showing none of the progress he'd made over the past months. "Actually, you've been absent-minded all night long. What's wrong?"

With a sigh, he slumped next to her on the bed. "I'm worried about a friend of mine."

"A friend? Do I know him? And what's wrong with him?"

He massaged his temple before elaborating. "Ralph. He's a hunter who took me under his wings when I first came to the compound. Last week, he took a team of young recruits on a hunt, and we haven't heard from him since. Ralph's skilled and careful. It's not like him not to check in for so long."

She bit her lip. "I'm sorry."

"We don't know for sure if anything happened. They might be too busy to contact us."

"Why don't you look for him?"

He rubbed the back of his neck. "I'd have to go alone, which would be reckless."

"What about your team?"

"Since I've spent no time in the field lately, I'm not part of any team anymore. My former colleagues are currently on another mission with a new team lead."

"Can't someone else check on them?"

"Theoretically, yes. But since it's not even been a week, management hasn't assigned anyone yet." He stood up and paced the room. "Hunters often vanish off the radar for several weeks. So, no other team will search for them until a month has passed.

"Ralph is more responsible than most and would not disappear without a word. Yet my superiors won't change our regulations just because I tell them it's unusual for him not to contact us. They won't stop me from looking for him, but leaving on my own is too risky."

She nodded. "If you're up against a vampire strong enough to bring down an entire team, you don't stand a chance without backup."

He stopped pacing and eyed her thoughtfully. "You'd have my back, wouldn't you?"

She chuckled. "Yes, but I doubt taking me as backup would comply with your regulations."

"Maybe not. Although I doubt there are rules prohibiting me from taking you on a hunt. Who in his right mind takes a vampire as backup?" He laughed a hollow laugh.

Her stomach fluttered. "Are you actually considering it?"

"Why not? With you by my side, we can take down any vampire."

At his words, a warm feeling spread in her chest. "I'd be happy to join you…as long as you don't get into trouble for taking me along."

A slight smile built on his lips. "I'll run this idea through the necessary channels first and then prepare for our departure. With some luck, we can leave tomorrow night."

****

If the worry about Ralph's fate hadn't dampened his mood, Dave would have reveled in the opportunity of taking Sarah on a road trip. Of course, his superiors only agreed because of the potential threat to Ralph's team.

With a forced smile, he entered Sarah's room and tossed her a bag of blood. "Are you up for a journey?"

"Anytime." She emptied the bag in under a minute. "Did they actually agree to let me join you?"

The sour face of the chairman flashed in front of his eyes. "I didn't leave them much of a choice when I insisted on investigating Ralph's disappearance. Since you've been a big help lately, they didn't come up with a good enough reason to keep me from bringing you along. We can leave right away if you're ready?"

"It's not like I had any other plans. A change in scenery sounds lovely." Her beautiful eyes sparkled.

"Since we'll be on the road for a few days, I already packed clothes and several bags of blood. Do you need anything else?"

She shook her head as a reply.

"Then let's go."

Like so many times before, he put the transport-helmet on her head and cuffed her wrists to comply with the compound's ridiculous security measures.

He led her down the stairs to the main hall, where an elevator brought them to the underground parking lot. They passed the hunting vans and several other cars before arriving at his black SUV. With tinted windows, a mesh dividing the front from the back, and silver hooks on the doors and between the seats to attach chains, the car transported vampires securely to and from the compound.

He opened the back door for her. Once she sagged into the soft leather seat, he removed the helmet and handcuffs. He didn't bother to chain her to the hooks. Even if his colleagues spotted them driving by, they wouldn't notice this detail.

"Hopefully, we can put some distance behind us before we have to rest. It's almost dawn, but these tinted windows are custom made and block out sunlight."

"Don't worry about the sun. I'll be fine," she said. "Where exactly are we going?"

"Ralph and his team were hunting somewhere in the northern part of Seattle. I know the hotel they stayed at, so we'll begin our investigation there."

"Seattle is quite far from here, isn't it?"

He nodded and took the driver's seat, stifling a yawn. "That's why we leave now. Make yourself comfortable in the back."

Although the sun rose when they left the underground parking lot, its rays didn't seem to bother her. Whenever he checked on her in the rearview mirror, she looked through the window with a dreamy expression on her face.

After about five hours on the road, his eyes threatened to fall shut. He got off the highway and parked in front of a homey two-story motel at the edge of a forest. "Let's rent a room and sleep for a few hours."

He exited the car, opened the door for her, and trudged toward the front desk.

"Aren't you coming?" he asked when she didn't follow him.

Did she expect him to chain her up again? He

sighed. "I will not restrain you while we're out. We both know you could break free whenever you want. And no one here would mind a vampire running around freely."

Without waiting for a reply, he entered the building. An older woman in a flowery dress greeted him at the reception. He returned her warm smile and asked for two rooms for the day.

Sarah caught up to him when the receptionist gave him two sets of keys for the motel's only vacant room.

He turned to her. "Sorry, they only had one vacancy—a double room with twin beds. I hope you don't mind sharing it with me?"

She stiffened. "Are you sure *you* don't mind? I could sleep in the car."

He frowned. Why would he mind sharing the room with a gorgeous woman? Then realization dawned on him. "I don't care what you are. And I won't let you sleep in the car."

The receptionist cleared her throat. "Should I lead you to your room, then?"

"Yes, please," he replied.

She brought them to a spacious but simple room on the second floor, which comprised two wooden beds with green linen, two nightstands with old-fashioned lamps, a small wardrobe, and an adjacent bathroom. A painting of a single white flower in a vase hung on the wooden wall. "Enjoy your stay."

Once they were on their own, Sarah curled up on a bed, hugging her knees to her body. "You shouldn't be so comfortable sharing a room with a vampire."

"I'm not sharing a room with just any vampire. I'm sharing it with you. And I trust you."

"Why? I'm still a monster."

He was about to enter the bathroom, but her words stopped him in his tracks. Shaking his head, he turned to look at her. "Don't put yourself down all the time. I don't see a vampire when looking at you. I see a beautiful, kind-hearted woman who has suffered far too much in her young life. Your actions prove you're not a monster, so don't depict yourself as one."

She drew in a breath and nodded.

He yearned to take her in his arms and comfort her, but they were on a mission. And despite all the time they'd spent together, she usually bolted or flinched when he got too close. Today wouldn't be any different, and he would not jeopardize their working relationship and her aspirations by giving in to unrequited desires. Before he did something he'd regret, he vanished into the bathroom to take a cold shower.

Ten minutes later, he returned, wearing nothing but boxer shorts. Her eyes scanned every inch of his body. When he grinned at her, she blushed and quickly averted her gaze.

"I didn't expect you to be so shy." He chuckled. Maybe the attraction was not completely one-sided. "I usually sleep in boxers, and I didn't think you'd mind."

"I don't," she blurted.

She wrapped herself into the covers of her bed and turned around to hide her flushed face. But he'd already seen enough.

Chapter 16

Knowing Dave slept in the same room kept Sarah awake. Her heart thundered in her chest as she listened to his rhythmic breathing. The earlier glimpse of his sculpted body, muscles accentuated by battle scars, spurred her imagination. What would they feel like beneath her fingers? And what would he taste like when she ran her tongue along his skin, looking for the perfect spot to sink her teeth into? She stilled at her own thought. His proximity enticed her mind and her inner beast, putting her on a path to dangerous territory. For his sake, she needed to quench her perilous longings.

After six hours of sleep for Dave and much less for her, they freshened up and continued their journey to Seattle. This time, Dave insisted she take the front seat by his side, like his colleagues would, instead of sitting in the back, where they'd transport vampires. She relented, although his proximity in this confined space increased her awareness of him even more. His spicy scent beguiled her senses, and warmth flooded her body. He was close enough to touch, and everything in her yearned for him. Yet she'd never give in to these urges. She was a monster, and thus not entitled to such feelings.

As Dave drove through the night with only a few short coffee breaks, they arrived just after dawn. He parked the car in front of an old brick building. Paint crumbled off the wall, and plywood covered a shattered window.

"This is the hotel where Ralph stayed."

"Doesn't look too inviting," she said. Funny how it still outclassed the dump she'd grown up in.

"We usually travel on a low budget. Hunting vampires doesn't pay well."

He exited the car and opened her door. She followed him to the building's entrance.

A keypad feigned security, but the door opened with a weak push. A stairwell led upstairs to the hotel's reception, which also served as a breakfast area. Several young people loafed on benches or stools, eating buttered toast. None looked like hunters.

"Excuse me"—he addressed the brunette woman behind the reception desk—"I'm looking for a couple of friends. They checked in about a week ago."

The receptionist pursed her lips. "We don't give out information on our customers."

"I understand," he said. "However, I haven't heard from them in days and I'm worried. I need to know if they are fine." He discreetly handed her a bill.

She sighed. "I'll see what I can do. Do you have a name for me?"

"Ralph…Smith."

She typed something on her computer. "Yes…They were traveling in a group of five. I remember them. They looked like trouble, carrying knives and other weapons. Your friend paid cash for ten days. I warned them not to cause any problems and handed them the keys for two family rooms."

"Could you do me a favor and check if they are in their rooms? And if not, could you check if there is anything…unusual in there?"

109

The receptionist nodded. "Wait here, please."

She picked up a spare key from below her desk and left. When she returned a few minutes later, a serious expression had replaced her smile. "Your friends weren't in their rooms. I've been here since four a.m., and I didn't see them leave, so I bet they weren't here all night. Do you think something happened? Should we call the cops?"

"Oh no, don't you worry. I'm sure they'll be back in no time. Actually, I think I'll wait here for them. Do you have two rooms for me and my friend for a few nights?"

The receptionist narrowed her eyes at Sarah. "I hope you won't cause any trouble, either. I only have a family room left. Or you can get bunk beds in one of the dorm rooms."

"We'll take the family room."

"Okay. Unfortunately, check-in isn't before two p.m."

"Could you make an exception? If it helps, we'll pay for last night as well."

After a moment of consideration, the receptionist agreed and led them to their room, which comprised a king-sized bed, two bunk beds, and nothing else—not even a bathroom.

"Well, you can have the king-sized bed," he offered.

Sarah shook her head. "I'm fine with a bunk bed. Besides, there's less light in the corner."

"Suit yourself. I'm too tired to argue."

He lay down on the bed and drifted off to sleep within minutes, still wearing his shirt and jeans. The slow up and down of his chest soothed her, and she followed him into the land of dreams.

He was still asleep when she woke. His face looked

so much more peaceful without worry lines, so she let him sleep. The sooner they found Ralph and his team, the quicker he could truly relax.

In order to investigate their disappearance, she tiptoed out of the hotel room. Maybe one of the other hotel guests or employees had noticed something?

No one occupied the reception, but a pair of backpackers lingered around a table, playing a game.

"What are you girls playing?"

"Chinese checkers," a skinny blonde with a New Zealand accent answered.

"We just finished this round, so you can join if you like," the other girl offered with a thick foreign accent, pushing her glasses up her nose.

"Oh no, thank you," Sarah said. "I don't even know the rules."

The girl with the glasses smiled warmly. "Don't worry, I just learned them myself. I'll explain them to you."

"Another time." She returned her smile. "I'm actually looking for my friends…They stayed here a few days ago."

"Well, I've been here for a week, so I might have seen them. What do they look like?"

Sarah didn't know Ralph or his team, but she'd seen enough hunters to give a general description. "They're traveling in a group of five—a middle-aged man with four adolescents. Since they're working out a lot, they might seem slightly intimidating. Their line of work usually keeps them up all night, so they often sleep during the day and keep to themselves."

"I've seen them." The girl with the New Zealand accent interrupted her.

Hope surged through her body. "When? Do you know where they went?"

"Four or five days ago. I overheard them talking about Gas Works Park."

"Gas Works Park?"

"It's a nearby park, less than thirty minutes by foot, built on the former site of a gasification plant. It's so worth a visit—you can check out the artistically changed remains of the plant there," the Kiwi girl said.

"Artistic? The park looks like a junkyard! There's nothing nice about those pieces of metal." The girl with glasses wrinkled her nose.

"I like it," the other girl said. "It's such a vast area with a magnificent view."

The two girls discussed the merits of the park, but she didn't pay attention any longer. She had the information she needed.

"There you are!" Dave's voice startled her.

She turned to him. "Did you sleep well?"

He nodded. "What were you up to?"

"Why, were you worried I'd run away?" she asked with a teasing smile.

"Not at all."

"I found us a clue. We should check out Gas Works Park."

After they had their respective breakfasts—a bag of blood for her and a sandwich from a convenience store for him—they headed to the park.

The last rays of the sun still colored the world in orange and red, and several people were walking their dogs or sitting on a blanket to enjoy the last days of summer. Yet everything seemed unusually quiet. A chill in the air unsettled her.

"Even if they were here, they're long gone. What did you hope to find?" he asked.

"Can't you feel the supernatural energy?"

He frowned. "What are you talking about?"

"Remnants of energy linger in the air. I also smell traces of blood. A fight took place here a couple of days ago." She tracked the scent to a structure of several copper barrels and scrutinized every piece.

Something metallic gleamed from a chink between two barrels. A knife? She bent down to pick it up and handed it to him. "Does this look familiar?"

"It's hard to tell."

"Either way, I think your colleagues fought a vampire here. The enormous amount of residual energy tells me he was old and powerful."

She roamed the site in search of more clues. Something about the supernatural energy gave her goosebumps. Suddenly, she froze.

"What is it?"

"I've had an ominous feeling ever since arriving at the park. Now I know why. This supernatural energy feels eerily familiar." She gulped. "I believe I've crossed paths with whoever attacked your friend…Probably before I became a vampire, which explains why I didn't recognize his energy at once."

"Who is it?"

"I don't know, but…I might be able to lure him here."

"Are you sure you want to?" He cleared his throat. "Face someone from your past, I mean."

She swallowed the lump in her throat. "I always knew I had to confront my past sooner or later. Let's get it over with."

Chapter 17

Despite the warm evening air, Sarah's fingers felt icy cold. Once all passersby had left the park, a sinking feeling settled in her stomach. It was time. She released the energy slumbering within her, letting it roam freely for the first time in months.

When the force of her power hit Dave, he winced.

"Powerful vampires rarely tolerate intruders in their hunting grounds, so he'll want to deal with me," she explained.

Her chest tightened as she paced around the copper structures. Was she ready to face her past?

"Who do we have here?" A familiar voice froze the blood in her veins. She turned around to find a tall, blond man with icy blue eyes about ten meters from her. *Vincent.*

He leaned against the metallic structure, with his hands stashed in the pockets of his black suit. "Aren't you the little runaway from our training program for new soldiers?"

All words escaped her, and her body trembled. The image of him baring his fangs and pressing her against a wall flashed across her mind.

"Have you come running back now?" He glanced at Dave. "And what's he doing here? A gift to regain my favor?"

"What?" Dave asked.

His voice snapped her out of her initial shock.

"Don't be ridiculous, Vincent." She spat on the ground. "Why would I ever want to return to the horrors you and your friends subjected me to?"

"Watch your mouth." He raised his voice and took a step toward her. "It's *Master Vincent* for you."

"I'm not a scared child for you to torture any longer."

"Maybe not, but you're a fledgling." He drew a saber. "I'll show you your place and teach you some respect."

She gulped. Vincent excelled with a saber—he'd taught her how to fight with one. And she was practically unarmed.

"Take my sword." Dave tossed his weapon to her.

"How cute…is the little vampire girl playing house with a hunter?" Vincent snorted.

Baring her fangs, she turned to Vincent. "This little vampire girl will kill you now."

He laughed. "I'd sure like to see you try."

She stormed at him. When their weapons clashed, his eyes widened with surprise.

"You've never seen me fight as a vampire. My strength has multiplied since you last humiliated me. And you no longer scare me."

With each slash, images of her horrible childhood surfaced and fueled her rage. Vincent locking her in a dark room and starving her because she didn't fight well enough. Vincent laughing as she lay on the ground, covered in bruises. And Vincent feeding on her until she lost consciousness from exhaustion and pain. She'd never forget his smug smile when he'd ordered her to fight her friend to the death.

Although he blocked her onslaught at first, her blows intensified with her growing anger. Soon, his whole body vibrated from the impact of her attacks. With a focused strike of the sword, she disarmed him.

With her subsequent slashes, she forced him farther and farther back, until a tree blocked his retreat. Panting, she pressed the blade against his throat.

"What kind of monster are you? Turning against the ones who made you…You'll forever be a fugitive, branded by your deeds against your own kind." He spat at her.

"*You* are the monster, and I was never on your side. *You* forced my obedience and turned me into what I hate." She balled her free fist at her side. "And they're not *my kind*. Let them come. If they hunt me down, they'll make it easier for me to kill every one of them. I'm starting with you tonight."

Snarling, he put a hand to her blade to push her away.

She pushed back, overpowered him, and severed his head with a clean cut. When it rolled to the ground, her knees gave in. She sank down, her body shivering.

****

"Are you all right?" Dave's heart ached to see her so broken.

When Sarah didn't react, he kneeled to hug her from behind, and a jolt ran through her body. "He can't hurt you anymore. You defeated him."

"He can't," she whispered. "But he's not the only monster. He mentioned a training program for new soldiers, and I can't help but wonder…are there children still going through the same ordeal somewhere?"

His jaw tensed. "Maybe. But we know about them

now, so we can save them."

"Yes, please." She shuddered. "I killed him before we could get any information about your friend. I'm sorry."

"It's okay. He wouldn't have told us anything, anyway. I'll search him for clues."

With a grimace, he approached the body and patted it down. He found a wallet with an ID card and a set of keys. "Maybe the keys open the door of whatever we find at the address on the ID? We should check it out."

She was still cowering on the ground.

If I could take her pain, I would. He squatted in front of her, searching her eyes. "If you need time, we can postpone the search until tomorrow."

"No." She inhaled deeply. "Just give me five minutes."

"Okay. In the meantime, I'll burn the body, so the authorities won't find any evidence of him."

"Wait," she said, and he stilled. "Let me get his saber—I wish to keep it."

"Why?"

"To remind myself I'm strong enough to defeat the tormentors from my past."

"Was he the one who turned you?" He swallowed.

"No. He was one of several vampires who enjoyed making our lives miserable. Although he fought well with a saber, the others often disregarded him. Maybe he found solace in our suffering."

"So, he let his negative emotions out on children? How despicable."

She shrugged. "All vampires are this way."

"Not all of them. You're different." He'd repeat it as many times as necessary. Until she believed it one day.

She smiled weakly at him.

****

Forty minutes later, they arrived at the address on the ID—a Victorian house with blue walls and a perfectly trimmed lawn on the outskirts of town.

"Can you tell if there are vampires inside?" Dave asked.

After concentrating on the building, Sarah shook her head. "I can't feel any supernatural beings. But they might hide their aura from me. I detect several humans, though."

"Do you think it's Ralph and the others?" He held his breath.

"I don't know. For now, we should assume they're Vincent's acquaintances."

"What do you propose we do?" he asked.

"I'll ring the doorbell. Whoever opens the door might assume I'm a friend of Vincent. We'll see where it goes from there."

"Okay. I'll stay here as your backup then."

She got out of the car and walked along the barely illuminated pathway to the front door. There was no name tag on the wall. She rang the bell and listened.

When no one answered the door after a few minutes of waiting, she gestured for him to join her. Once he arrived, she whispered, "Let's see if one of the keys works."

He nodded and fetched the keys from his pocket. The second one fit perfectly, and the door opened with a creak. They waited a few seconds. When everything stayed quiet, they sneaked inside and inspected the house. It was empty.

"Didn't you say you felt humans in here?"

"I still feel them." She bit her lower lip. "Is there a hidden basement or something?"

When they split up to search the rooms again, she discovered a trapdoor below an armchair. She opened it and climbed down a ladder to a hidden dungeon drenched in darkness. Even with no light, she discerned several cells, most of them empty. Four humans lay on the ground in four of them, their hands and feet shackled. They didn't react to her presence.

"Dave? You should come down here," she called. "Bring a flashlight or something."

He entered the dungeon two minutes later. When the light of his smartphone revealed the shape of a human, he gasped. She also recognized Ethan, the teenager with the dragon tattoo she fought in her first training session.

"Is he alive?" he asked.

"Yeah. His heart is beating, just like the hearts of the other three humans. They are most likely unconscious from blood loss, exhaustion, and dehydration." Apart from Ethan, she also recognized the second boy and the girl from the same training. The fourth youth was a girl with long, red hair.

"Let's call an ambulance and get them upstairs," he suggested in a quiet, feeble tone. Had he realized the hard truth? With only these four down here, Ralph was most likely dead.

Vincent's keys opened the cell doors and the shackles on the prisoners. They carried the youths upstairs and placed them carefully on the living room floor.

The second boy stirred and opened his eyes. "Dave…"

"Yes, Alex, I'm here," Dave said. "You're safe

now."

Alex trembled as he struggled for words. "Ralph…is dead. The vampire was…playing with us. We never should have…"

"Shush, it's all right." He took the boy's hand, but his expression faltered.

Loud sirens announced the ambulances. She opened the front door for them.

"What happened?" a paramedic asked.

"I don't know," Dave said. "We found the four of them like this. I believe they lost a lot of blood."

The paramedic narrowed his eyes at them. "The police will question you later."

He and his colleagues examined the four young hunters. After loading the youths into the ambulances, they left for the hospital.

Sarah and Dave stayed behind. Prior to driving back to the hotel for some much-needed sleep, Dave called the hunters' association to ask them to handle the formalities.

Chapter 18

"Please, I'm hungry and tired. I can't fight no more." Hot tears streamed down Sarah's face as she lay flat on the cold ground, struggling to keep her eyes open.

"Shut up and pick up the sword," a merciless voice ordered.

"Please, Master Vincent. My entire body hurts." She whimpered.

"Stop whining." Steps approached her. She gasped when Master Vincent kicked her in the rips. "I'm not here to babysit you. Get up. If you can't stand, I'll turn you into my next meal."

She rolled onto her side and pushed her hands into the ground to lift herself up. But her frail body couldn't carry her weight, and she collapsed.

"Disappointing." He pulled her up by her hair.

She didn't even possess the energy to scream out in pain as Master Vincent pressed her against a wall and sank his fangs into her flesh.

A hand shaking her shoulder woke Sarah. She blinked at Dave, who leaned over her, his face inches from hers.

"Are you okay?" he asked.

She sat up slowly in her bunk bed and took a deep breath to calm herself. "Nothing more than a bad dream. I'm okay now."

"Really?"

His enticing scent washed over her, and her mouth watered.

"Yeah. At least once I eat breakfast." Holding her breath, she pushed to her feet and grabbed a bag of blood from the cooler.

Since neither of them felt like sleeping anymore, they got dressed and drove to the hospital to check on the four young hunters.

A nurse informed them the youths suffered from high blood loss and dehydration, but they were responding well to the treatment. She led them to the room where the four were sleeping and warned them not to wake the patients.

Quietly, they waited in the chairs near the youths' bedsides.

After more than an hour, the girl with the red hair woke up.

"Where am I?" she murmured sleepily.

Sarah walked to her. "Morning." She smiled at the girl, making sure not to show her teeth. "You're at the hospital. We saved you last night."

The girl looked at her and squinted her eyes. "Do I know you? You seem familiar somehow…"

She bit her lip. Telling her she was a vampire would probably scare the poor girl. She glanced at Dave, who slouched absentmindedly in his chair. "Dave?"

His gaze focused on them. He got up and joined her.

The girl relaxed when she recognized him.

"Hello, Amanda. How are you?" he asked.

"I've been better." Amanda grimaced. "What happened?"

"Since we hadn't heard from your team in almost a week, Sarah and I went looking for you. Our investigation led us to Gas Works Park, where we stumbled across a blond vampire. After Sarah defeated him, we checked out his home address and found you."

Amanda looked at her with wide eyes. "You defeated him on your own?"

She simply nodded.

Dave sighed. "Sarah is the vampire who's been training with our recruits for months."

"I'll leave if you're uncomfortable with me being here," she added.

Amanda shook her head. "Don't be ridiculous. Dave said you saved me, so I'm grateful for your presence."

Sarah looked away, rubbing her forearms.

He cleared his throat. "I know you've been through a lot, but since you're the first one awake, could you tell us more about what happened?"

Amanda nodded slowly and inhaled audibly. "We were...excited to join Ralph on this hunt—our second mission ever. Rumors about people vanishing in Northern Seattle brought us here to investigate. Witnesses reported people disappearing during late-night walks in Gas Works Park, which is where we headed on our third night.

"There, the vampire approached me, dressed like a businessman in a fine suit. He asked what we were doing in the park in the middle of the night." She gritted her teeth. "I didn't realize what he was, but Ralph did. He screamed at me to get away and charged at him. The vampire dodged his blade. We also drew our weapons and attacked the monster, but to no avail. He was...playing with us, laughing as if he was having a blast. Faster than we could react, he killed Ralph by ripping his heart from his chest."

Dave gasped.

Amanda's voice broke as she continued. "I'm not sure what happened then…It's all a blur in my mind. The next thing I remember is waking up in that cell."

"Do you know why he captured you?" Sarah asked.

Amanda shuddered. "He said he liked our youth and our fighting spirit…and he planned to turn us after enjoying our blood for a while."

She swallowed hard. "So, he was looking for new soldiers."

"What do you mean?" Amanda asked.

"He kidnapped me as a child and tortured me for years to turn me into a vampire soldier."

"And apparently he succeeded," Amanda whispered.

"Not the way he'd hoped." She forced a smile.

"And he won't hurt anyone ever again." Dave's gaze locked with hers.

Amanda relaxed on the bed, and a yawn escaped her. "I'm glad."

"We'll leave, so you can rest," Dave said. "Sleep well. You're safe now."

****

On the drive back to the hotel, Dave's gaze wandered to Sarah every chance he got. The events of the previous two nights underlined how much she'd suffered. The horrors she'd faced exceeded everything he'd imagined. And despite her past, she sacrificed her freedom and suppressed her urges so she could protect humans, fighting for a better future for them. How admirable.

Once they arrived, she flopped onto her bed, staring at the ceiling.

"Sarah." Even if she continued maintaining a distance between them, he'd give everything to support her.

He sat on the bed and waited till her eyes settled on him. "You said Vincent wasn't the only vampire who aimed to turn kids into vampire soldiers, didn't you?"

She nodded. "There were three others like him, torturing us for fun and talking about creating soldiers for their royal family."

"Royal family? You mentioned them before. Who are they?"

"An elite group of vampires who reign over my...their kind. From what I understand, Vincent and the others respected and feared them."

"I'll help you bring all of them down." Ready to pledge his life to her and become her knight in shining armor, he placed his hand on his chest above his heart. He caught her eyes in an intense stare, and her breath hitched. "Your tormentors and the royal family...let's make them pay for what they did...and protect others from the same fate. Although I'm not as powerful as you, I'll stay by your side and devote everything to you and your cause...if you want me to?"

Tears welled up in her eyes at his promise. "Yes, please."

He scooted closer to her and took her into his arms. She froze at the contact.

"You don't have to be strong all the time," he said. "You're not alone anymore."

Hesitantly, she melted into his embrace and sobbed.

Part II

REBIRTH

Newfound perception
through the eyes of another.
Can evil turn good?

Chapter 19

Clouds shrouded the moon as Dave meandered through the streets of Downtown LA. The rising number of missing persons reports combined with rumors about disturbing noises like screams and crying coming from an abandoned apartment complex justified an investigation by the hunters' association, or in this case, him.

Instead of searching the building directly and scaring the perpetrators into fleeing, he hoped to lure them out by walking the streets on his own, posing as bait.

His hair stood on end as he passed derelict houses, walls smeared with graffiti, and poorly lit alleyways. No sane person would walk these streets alone at this hour. Of course, he was not truly alone. Sarah was hiding nearby.

Despite his vow to help her take revenge, they'd made no progress in the past year. He'd hoped to find clues during hunting missions and thus volunteered to return to the field with her as backup. She never strayed far from his side, accompanying him wherever he went. Together, they killed countless vampires. Yet none had provided a connection to her past.

As he took another turn, a young woman with

shoulder-length, brown curls, wearing a dirty sweater, exited a large apartment house and looked around. Once she spotted him, a calculating smile crossed her lips, and she hurried toward him. With her unnaturally pale skin and the aura surrounding her, Dave recognized her as a vampire.

He stiffened slightly, unable to hide his instinctual reaction. Still, he forced a smile. "Are you all right, miss?"

She shook her head and shuddered. "I-I think there's someone in my flat. Please, you seem…trustworthy. Could you come along and check for me?"

He raised an eyebrow. If this was how they usually got their victims, the humans had it coming. Who in his right mind would offer to face an intruder instead of calling the cops? No one deserved to die for their stupidity, though. "Someone broke into your flat? Don't worry, I know karate. I'll chase him off for you."

A relieved smile spread across her face. "Thank you! Please, follow me."

She led him into the building, which could serve as the setting for a horror movie. Lights flickered in the foyer, part of the tapestry had been torn off, and an "Out of order" sign blocked the elevator. Dried blood stained the carpet, and the wooden stairs creaked as they ascended to the second floor.

"My apartment is the second door on the left." She stayed at the top of the stairs, waiting for him to inspect her home.

He smiled at her encouragingly and opened the door with his left hand while his right one clasped the silver dagger in his coat pocket.

The light inside the apartment was off, and the

switch did not work. Yet a window on the opposite wall illuminated enough of the entry hallway for him to make out five doors. All of them were closed, so he decided to check them one by one.

The first door on his left opened with a squeal and revealed a living room. Dave froze when he spotted two male vampires lounging on a corduroy fabric couch, sucking blood from the lifeless body of a middle-aged woman.

One of them, a young man with blond locks, looked up from his meal, and a wide grin spread across his dimpled face. "Nice. Kasey brought us seconds."

Slowly, Dave retreated a few steps.

"No, no, don't run." The blond vampire got to his feet.

The other vampire, an older man with a full beard, only grunted. His mouth never left the victim he was chewing on.

Dave's back bumped into the handle of the front door as the blond vampire caught up to him with long strides.

Keeping the door shut with one hand and blocking Dave's way with his other, the vampire smirked. "We're having a party, and you're our guest of honor. So, I'm afraid I can't let you leave."

A muffled scream from outside drew the vampire's attention away from him. He used the distraction to pull his blade out of his coat and plunge it into his heart.

"Wha—?" The vampire gasped and stared at Dave with incredulous eyes before the light left them and he slumped onto the floor.

Roused by his companion's death, the bearded vampire tackled Dave. "How dare you? I'll make you pay!"

"Why? You were the ones planning to eat me."

The vampire growled and snapped at his neck.

Holding his arms in front of his upper body like a shield, he used all his strength to keep the rabid beast away from his throat.

The front door opened while they tussled. Sarah tiptoed into the room, but the bearded vampire only focused on Dave's neck and didn't notice her approach.

With a stroke of her saber, she severed his head from behind.

"Thanks," Dave whispered. "We still need to check the other rooms."

"Okay. I'll follow your lead."

With shaking hands, he opened the next door to find a small storage room. The remaining door on the left revealed a kitchen, while a bathroom was behind the first one on the right. The last door was locked. Moans and grunts sounded from within.

He exchanged a glance with her and stepped aside. She threw herself against the door, breaking it. She practically flew into the room, landing on all fours in front of an enormous bed. Once she lifted her gaze, her body froze, and her cheeks turned red.

He entered to see what she was looking at. A man and a woman, both vampires, were going at it. Lost in the heat of passion, they hadn't even noticed the intrusion.

Sarah also seemed mesmerized by the sight.

When he whispered her name, she blinked at him. Then she drew her saber, tiptoed to the end of the bed, and jumped on it, piercing the hearts of both vampires with one thrust of her weapon.

"At least they died happy," he suggested.

"Uh-huh. I'll check the other apartments." She left without looking at him.

He sighed. He'd love to experience the same fire with her, but he still hadn't torn down the walls she'd built between them. At least she didn't shy away from his every touch anymore. What she needed most was a loyal friend, not a lover. So, he hadn't confessed his feelings. There was too much at stake if things didn't work out.

She returned to inform him the remaining apartments were empty.

They rounded up the bodies and doused them with gasoline to torch them and this godforsaken apartment house.

After exiting the building, he fetched a box of matches from his pants pocket to set it ablaze. He still fumbled with a match when the sound of slow, deliberate clapping caused his heart to sink.

Chapter 20

Sarah tensed and drew her saber, scanning the area to pinpoint the source of the clapping.

A tall vampire with shoulder-length, dark-brown hair stood on top of another vacated building on the other side of the currently deserted street, a sword stashed beneath his black leather coat. Her gut tightened when his old, potent aura combined with an unusual, smothering energy washed over her.

He studied her with a dark smile on his lips. "You gave us quite a show…Very entertaining."

"Get as far away as possible while I distract him," she whispered to Dave.

"Your human companion is of no interest to us—as long as he doesn't interfere." A light voice sounded from behind, startling her.

A young female vampire in black, with long, blonde hair in a braid, crouched on top of the building they'd just cleared. Unlike the man, she didn't feel old. Yet the same unusual power emanated from her.

Sarah hadn't noticed either of them before they spoke up. An icy shiver ran through her body at the thought of facing two vampires capable of fooling her this way.

"Don't worry, as long as we put on a good show, you'll only fight me." The young woman smiled, showing her fangs.

Sarah chewed on her lip. Could the female read her mind? And what did she mean by putting on a good show?

"What the hell do you want from us?" Dave drew his gun and aimed at the man.

He pursed his lips, but otherwise ignored the gun pointed at him. "From you? Nothing. If you sit still and watch, no harm will come to you. We're more interested in your…pet."

"My what?" Dave asked.

"Your companion. You put a collar around her neck, didn't you? So, calling her your pet isn't far-fetched," the vampire explained with a grin.

"What the hell?" Not caring about exposing her back to the woman, Sarah stormed at him.

He watched her approach calmly without so much as moving a muscle. Why didn't he prepare for her impending attack?

The female appeared in front of her, blocking the way with a silver staff. "I told you *I'm* your opponent…I can relate to hating the term 'pet,' though."

"What do you want?" She gritted her teeth.

"For now, we wish to watch you fight," the man answered. "Lilah has eagerly awaited a chance to test her strength against yours. Given your similar backgrounds, I am curious to see who'll win."

"Similar backgrounds? What do you mean?" Had she been part of one of the training units Vincent had mentioned? Forced to become a monster?

Lilah shook her head. "Although I also trained hard and fed on vampire blood long before I was turned, I'm not like you. I chose this life."

She gaped at her. "Why would anyone choose this

life?"

"Freedom, power, and love. And so many other reasons. I've never felt like I belonged anywhere until I stumbled into his world. But I'm not here to talk."

She wouldn't associate words like freedom, power, and love with vampirism. All she'd encountered while growing up was oppression, helplessness, and torture. Images of her captors' cruelty and the deaths of her almost sisters flooded her mind. No, she couldn't relate to the woman's attitude at all.

When she glanced at Dave, he holstered his gun and retreated to the entrance of the building they'd cleared. He probably realized these vampires played in another league. Would they really leave him alone? The fear of losing him to these monsters clutched her chest.

She took another look at her opponent. Lilah was suppressing her strength. Like a wild animal, she crouched on the ground. Her silver staff reflected the moonlight of the now clear sky.

Lilah's eyes bore into hers. Was she merely assessing her, or was she reading her mind? Such advanced abilities should be impossible for someone so young.

Sarah's stomach quivered. She had little experience in battling vampires with special abilities. They didn't leave her much of a choice, though.

Once she moved toward her, Lilah began spinning her staff, deflecting every stab and blow of her saber. Even when she feigned a strike from the right, spun around, and attacked from above, Lilah easily sidestepped her, as if she knew her every move. Could she foresee her actions?

"Come on, I'm sure you can do more. Show me your

true strength," Lilah said.

How does she know I'm holding back? For fear of losing control, she never tapped into the dark energy slumbering within her. Yet the risk of losing against this opponent was more imminent. Concentrating on herself for a moment, she released her ironclad hold on her power, letting it flow through her body.

Lilah's eyes bulged in surprise when Sarah charged at her with full force. When the saber clashed with her staff, a wide smile built on her face. "Much better. Now, let's have some fun!"

"Fun?" Sarah echoed in disbelief. She'd never call fighting for her life fun.

"If you're not having fun, you're doing something wrong. And what could be more fun than fighting a strong opponent and pushing past your limits?"

She groaned as the powerful thrusts of Lilah's staff vibrated through her. Tightening the grip on her saber, she struck back. "How about killing monsters like you?"

"What a destructive attitude." Lilah pouted. "If your aim is to kill, you need to try a lot harder."

"Be careful what you wish for," she growled.

With a loud *clang*, she blocked Lilah's attack with both hands on her blade, then spun around and slashed swiftly at her opponent.

Lilah gracefully evaded the blade. "Your intentions are too obvious."

She snarled as something primal inside of her screamed to be released. Blood pounded in her ears, and adrenaline rushed through her body. But she would not give in to the beast. Gritting her teeth, she fought her inner darkness as well as her opponent.

No matter how much strength or speed she used,

Lilah dodged or fended everything off. Whenever Lilah struck back, she parried, but the attacks were taking a toll on her. Did her moves have a similar effect?

"I've seen enough," the male vampire suddenly announced.

Lilah immediately ceased fighting, but she didn't care. Why should she listen to the vampire? Her opponent's hesitation might be the opening she'd waited for. She swung her blade at the woman, who ducked just in time.

"Sarah…" Dave's voice caught her attention.

When she turned around, her stomach dropped, and the blood froze in her veins.

He stood in front of the building roughly ten meters from her. The male vampire loomed right behind him, his sword pressed against Dave's throat.

Chapter 21

"Very well." The male vampire smiled. "Since I've got your attention now, I—"

"Let him go," Sarah shouted.

He sighed. "I'm not interested in your hunter friend. In fact, I'll release him right now if you drop your weapon and listen to what I have to say."

Would he keep his word? Everything in her screamed not to trust him, but what choice did she have? With his age, his power might surpass the female's. If they combined their strength, they could easily overpower and kill her. So why didn't they? With Dave's life at stake, listening to them was her only option. She nodded and slowly put her saber on the ground.

As promised, the man let go of Dave and sheathed his sword. "Go."

With shaking limbs, Dave walked over to her.

"Are you all right?" she asked.

He trembled slightly. "Yeah."

She squeezed his arm for a moment to comfort him, assure herself of his safety, and ease the tension in her gut.

"Lilah," the vampire called his female companion. She appeared next to him, going down on one knee while keeping her eyes trained on Sarah.

"You're talking about freedom, but all I see is subservience. Listening to his every command and kneeling in front of your master…How pathetic," she scoffed.

Lilah broke into laughter. "You're so clueless, it's cute." She got to her feet. "Don't misunderstand our relationship. It's good manners to honor your sire and act respectful while interacting with other vampires. Cain doesn't even care about these formalities. I do, because I love him and I'm grateful for everything he's done for me. So, I act accordingly."

Cain cleared his throat. "Anyway, we're here to make you an offer."

"One you shouldn't decline," Lilah added.

"We're not from around here," he said. "Our king sent us from Europe with two *very* different missions. Which one we fulfill depends on you."

"On me?" She drew her eyebrows together.

Lilah took a few steps toward her. "We needed to see if you're as powerful as the rumors say. A child who grew up training, with a steady intake of our blood. They say your strength equaled that of a mediocre vampire by the time you were a teenager." Her eyes sparkled. "Your story inspired me to transcend my human limits long before I became a vampire. Of course, being turned multiplied my strength even more. I'm sure it was the same for you. Still, we had to find out whether you possessed the same potential."

"Why?"

"Because it's essential for choosing our mission," Cain answered.

"Our official mission is to kill you," Lilah said bluntly. "The alternative is to join forces and to help you bring down the American royal family—if you are strong enough."

"Join forces with me?" Disbelief colored her voice. "Why would you even assume I'd be willing to fight by your side? And why are you interested in bringing the royal family down?"

"Politics," said Cain. When she frowned, he elaborated. "You are strong, but you can't kill all of them by yourself. Your chances won't improve even if your hunter friend helps you. Truth be told, he's a liability and your weak spot, as we've just proven. Turning our offer down is no option for you."

When she opened her mouth to argue, Lilah chimed in. "Think about it before you say something you'd regret. As of now, you don't stand a chance against us. Yet we're offering our support."

"Why?" Dave asked.

"I don't know what you know about the relationship between the American and European vampires, but it's not good. We're worried about the way vampires act over here. There is no order and no respect. In the few weeks we've spent in North America, we've seen them torture and kill humans needlessly while leaving behind big messes." Cain clenched his fists. "This unnecessary display of violence draws too much unwanted attention to our existence and endangers all of us. Thus, weakening the vampires here in America is in our favor."

Their logic sounded reasonable, which is why she didn't trust them. Vampires thrived in a world full of cruelty, manipulation, and violence. Why would they be any different? Besides, she loathed their attitude. She'd rather bathe in a pool of liquid silver than work with them.

"We can also help you reach your full potential," Lilah said. "You still fight like a human."

"What?" Her nostrils flared.

"Don't get me wrong. Your strength and speed are extraordinary, and you wield your weapon well. You'll win against most vampires. It's not enough if you're up against the elite, though."

"What do you expect?" She huffed. "I've been a vampire for barely two years."

"Your age is not the problem. You suppress your instincts, even though they are a vampire's greatest advantage. And you don't possess any psychic abilities. Of course, no one taught you after your rebirth, but it's a waste of your potential."

Her assessment was spot on. So far, strength and speed had brought down the vampires she faced. But if more opponents like Cain and Lilah awaited her, she'd lose eventually.

"You don't have to decide now," Cain said. "Think about it, or discuss it with your hunter friend."

"What happens if she declines?" Dave asked.

"Then we'll have to choose mission number one," Lilah said matter-of-factly.

"You're not giving her much of a choice," Dave noted.

Lilah shrugged. "She can fight us. If she can't defeat us, she'll never bring her nemeses down on her own."

"We'll give you three days to decide," Cain said.

He offered Lilah his hand. She took it, and they teleported away.

Sarah winced when Dave punched the wall of the abandoned apartment building.

"Are you okay?" she asked.

He took a few shaky breaths before nodding. "Let's return for now. We can talk tomorrow, after thinking things through and getting some sleep."

****

Back at the compound, sleep eluded Dave. The encounter with the two vampires played again and again in his head, and the memory still chilled his bones. He'd been powerless, and his weakness put Sarah at risk once more.

After several restless hours, he got up, took a shower, and fetched a cup of coffee and a bag of blood from the kitchen before heading to Sarah's room.

"What will you do now?" Taking her hand in his, he sat down on the bed next to her.

She met his gaze, and her face reflected the turmoil inside of her. "I'm not sure I have a choice."

"So, you can't beat them?"

"Not if they combine their strength." She bit her lip. "Even if I only fought against the female, she'd have to make a mistake for me to gain the upper hand. And then there's her mysterious companion. We know he sired her, so we can assume he's more powerful than her."

"Unfortunately, I agree. Even if we fight together, we don't stand a chance against them." In fact, she was better off without him in a battle against such powerful foes.

A sad smile formed on her face. "I don't think anyone could help me fight those two."

"How about we stay here and never face them?"

She chuckled. "As much as I like the idea, I doubt I could run from them. They might have followed us here, waiting nearby for my decision. I wouldn't put it past them to destroy the compound to get to me. And I won't risk the lives of you and the other hunters."

"Good point." He sighed. "So, what about their

offer?"

"It sounds too good to be true. Helping me reach my full potential and bring down the most powerful vampires in America? I don't fully understand their reasoning. And I don't trust them because they're vampires."

"You forget you're a vampire, too."

"Oh, I never forget that." Her expression darkened, and his heart contracted in his chest in response. "I don't trust any vampire—myself included. But why would they lie? Even though I hate to admit it, they could have killed us last night."

"Yes. When he appeared right behind me, putting his sword to my throat without giving me time to react, I expected him to kill me." He shuddered. "But he didn't. He released me without a scratch."

"So, maybe they were telling the truth. Even if they made quite a show of it."

"Do you believe they could help you become stronger and reach your potential?"

She looked away, rubbing her forearms.

"Possibly," she admitted after a while. "I keep a lot of my power locked away because I'm afraid of losing control. If they showed me how to conquer the beast in me and taught me new abilities…"

"…then you could take revenge." He finished the sentence for her.

"What would you do?"

From a hunter's perspective, he should tell her not to trust them and to fight them with everything she'd got. Yet he said, "Their offer sounds like a once-in-a-lifetime opportunity. Trusting these vampires is risky, but who knows…They might surprise you and change your world completely. Just like you did for me."

He smiled at her, and a comforting warmth spread through his chest. She'd changed everything he thought he knew about vampires and exceeded his expectations time and time again.

She frowned for a moment before her eyes widened and a blush appeared on her cheeks.

"Whatever you decide, I'll support your decision." He squeezed her hand. "And I'll stay by your side if you want me to."

"Are you sure? We might not return for a while if we take them up on their offer."

"I promised to support you, didn't I? So, I'll stay with you for as long as you want and help you defeat your demons." Besides, there was nowhere else he'd rather be.

Tears glistened in her eyes. "Thank you."

Chapter 22

When Sarah awoke around dusk two nights later, a vibrant, supernatural aura greeted her from a distance—a blatant invitation from Lilah and Cain.

Based on the origin of their energy, they were approximately thirty miles north of the compound. Reason enough for her to prepare before they came to get her.

She took a quick shower, put on a tracksuit, and packed a travel bag. Dave entered her room soon after, also ready for departure. Despite their intention to take the vampires up on their offer, they armed themselves to the teeth.

She kept shifting in her seat as he drove them in his car, following her directions. The closer they got, the more her chest tightened. Was she doing the right thing? Wasn't it better to fight them until her last breath?

Dave's knuckles whitened while clutching the steering wheel.

"Are we close?" he asked. "The road ends up there."

"Yeah, we can walk from here."

He parked the car, and they took a hiking trail leading into a forest. With every step, the supernatural energy in the air grew more potent, causing her hair to stand on end.

After hiking for half an hour, they reached a clearing with a picnic area surrounded by wildflowers. Cain chilled on a table, his feet dangling in the air, while Lilah cuddled up to him, with her head on his lap. Why were they so relaxed?

She tightened her hand on the hilt of her saber as she approached them. "We're willing to accept your offer."

Lilah sat up with a yawn.

"*We?*" Cain asked. "Our offer pertains only to you—it's not meant for your ball and chain."

"We're a package deal," she said.

"He'll get you killed, you know."

She shook her head. "I taught him how to fight. He can bring down vampires by himself."

"Weak ones," Lilah said. "He's still too human, which makes him much too fragile."

"What do you mean by 'still too human'? He *is* human, and he'll *stay* human," she said decisively.

Lilah rolled her eyes. "With your history, you should know how to help someone surpass human limits without turning them."

"What are you suggesting?" Dave asked.

"Blood. Strengthen your body and heighten your senses by consuming ours. Then you might not be completely useless."

"Unacceptable," Sarah interjected.

"Why? Because blood tastes disgusting to a human? Like you, I've consumed vampire blood for years. The power you gain is well worth it. And it's not like drinking our blood would turn him," Lilah argued.

"I'll do it," he said.

She gaped at him. How could he willingly agree to drink the cursed liquid running through their veins?

"You've fed me your blood before to heal me. Why shouldn't we do this?"

"At least one of you is in his right mind." Lilah smirked. "Consuming the blood of three powerful vampires will give you quite a boost."

"Do you think you should offer *our* blood so freely?" Cain arched a brow at Lilah.

She shrugged. "I doubt she plans to turn him, so it doesn't really matter."

"What doesn't matter? Is there anything unusual about your blood?" Dave asked.

"Tasting our blood is a privilege," Cain said.

"Why? Does it have anything to do with the unusual power you emit?" Sarah asked.

"Oh, you can feel it?" Lilah glanced at her sire, who nodded. "As a matter of fact, there is a connection between our blood and this energy. It signifies our connection to the royal family."

The royal family? She took a step back. Was this a poor joke?

Lilah chuckled. "Relax. I'm not talking about the American one. We're part of the European royal family. The energy you're feeling warns other vampires to show us the respect we're due. You're the first one from around here to notice it, though. Maybe the others are not aware of its meaning, or they're not as perceptive as you, which is a good thing, because we're here unofficially."

"Enough about us," Cain said. "If you're serious about bringing the American royal family down, we'll train you."

"If you believe we require more training, why team up with us? Can't you extinguish them on your own?" Dave asked.

"Aren't you a clever one?" Lilah narrowed her eyes at him. "Our aim is to weaken them—without starting a war. To keep our role in their annihilation secret, we need your girlfriend here as some sort of…scapegoat."

Heat rose to her cheeks. "I'm not his…girlfriend."

Lilah ignored her comment. "With rumors about your strength and the vendetta you've got against your own kind, no one would question you're responsible for bringing the royal family down—unless you die halfway through the mission. So, we intend to make sure you don't."

"If we've answered all questions to your satisfaction, we should go." Cain hopped off the table and held out his hands invitingly.

"Where to?" she asked.

"You'll see."

Did she trust them enough to go along with them? While she pondered her options, Dave took Cain's left hand. She couldn't let him leave alone. Despite the queasy feeling in her gut, she followed his example by taking the other one.

Different energies swirled around her as Cain teleported them. The journey lasted less than three seconds, during which she clung to his hand as if it were the only thing keeping her from falling into an endless abyss. Even after her feet touched back on the ground, her body tingled from the aftereffects.

Although teleportation was nothing new to Sarah, it felt different from the times her tormentors had teleported her to remote training sites. Of course, nothing had ever been the same since they turned her into a monster.

They appeared in front of a small wooden cabin surrounded by lots of trees, literally in the middle of nowhere. Fern, moss, and red cedar trees shaped most of the environment.

"We bought this place a few days ago. No one will disturb our training here," Cain explained.

"Are you prepared for human visitors?" Dave asked with a hint of worry in his voice.

"You can get fresh water from the taps. The previous owners stocked the fridge with a few basics, and if you crave anything else, we'll buy groceries in a nearby city."

"Would you happen to have any blood bags stashed here as well?" she asked.

Lilah's chuckle startled her. Had the female teleported here on her own shortly after they had? Why did she possess such skills at her age?

"You don't need blood bags. I'll take you hunting if you're hungry," Lilah offered.

"I don't hunt for blood."

"You *will* hunt," Cain said. Before she could argue, he added, "You require fresh blood if you wish to become stronger. Bagged blood quenches your thirst, but it keeps you weak. We'll make sure you don't hurt anyone."

She nibbled on her lower lip. She hadn't fed on a human in over a year. If it was up to her, she'd never succumb to her primal urges again. She'd already hurt too many innocent people in her first weeks as a vampire before she'd learned to suppress her never-ending thirst.

"I assume you've fed tonight? So, postpone your worrying to tomorrow. Now, we'll train. Let's split up. You're with me while Lilah focuses on your friend. Follow me." Without awaiting a reply, he headed deeper into the forest.

Her gaze darted between Cain, Dave, and Lilah, and

her chest tightened. Could she leave him with her?

"He's safe with me. I promise," Lilah said.

"I don't find the words of a vampire very reassuring."

Dave sighed. "I'll be fine. Just go."

After another glance at him, she hurried after Cain.

Chapter 23

"Why did we split up? I'd prefer staying close to Dave," Sarah said once she caught up to Cain.

The trees in this area grew farther apart, allowing the moon to illuminate their surroundings. A creek snaked through the shrubs, and the whooshing of the water unnerved her.

"Your friend's presence distracts you. I need you to focus on yourself."

And worrying about him wouldn't distract her?

She sighed. "What do you want me to do?"

"You spend so much energy suppressing your true power. Embrace it instead. Let it flow freely, and then attack me."

Could she embrace her dark power without falling prey to the beast within? If she learned how to control it, she'd be one step closer to defeating her enemies.

She gulped and closed her eyes to concentrate.

When she released the hold on her power, a wave of energy swashed through her body, and she shuddered. Despite the quiver in her stomach, she drew her saber and charged at Cain.

He blocked with his sword. "Again."

She spun around and hurled herself at him, but he fended her off without breaking a sweat.

"Your attacks won't amount to anything unless you use your power to its full extent," he said.

"I am using my full power."

"No. You keep part of it locked inside your body. Instead of embracing it as part of yourself, you treat it like something dangerous. As long as you fear your own power, you can't use it properly."

"I'm not scared of anything." She snarled and slashed her saber at him.

His sword clashed with her weapon. "At the very least, you haven't accepted yourself. Your hatred of what you are is tearing you apart."

"Don't talk like you know me."

The next time she swung her weapon at him, he dodged, spun around, and then kicked her wrist with full force. Her saber clattered to the ground as pain shot through her bones.

"Kidnapped by monsters and tortured for years. Eventually turned into the creature you detest. Killing someone you cared about because of your uncontrollable thirst. Does that sound familiar?" he asked.

When she nodded slowly, he continued. "It's *my* story. I've lived this cursed life for over four hundred years. Don't assume you're the only vampire who's suffered at the hands of others."

Was he telling the truth? Or was it nothing but a ruse to gain her trust? And how had he learned about her past?

"Can you read my mind?" she asked.

"No, I only read intentions."

"Then how do you know so much about me?"

"Lilah caught glimpses of your memories. She can read minds as long as her target doesn't actively resist her. Apparently, your mind is an open book. It's something we need to rectify as well."

She gaped at him. "Isn't she around the same age as

me in vampire years? How can she possess more skills than you if you're her sire?"

"You're asking too many questions." He stashed his sword. "But understanding the difference between the two of you might help. Unlike you, Lilah has embraced her new nature. She enjoys every aspect of being a vampire, exploring her power to the fullest. In addition, not only my blood is flowing through her veins. Before I turned her, she consumed the blood of several powerful vampires, allowing her to tap into a variety of special abilities. With your similar background, the same potential slumbers in you if you embrace it—which brings us back to your lesson."

She chewed on her lower lip.

"I understand your reluctance," he said. "Becoming a vampire broke me. Only the wish for revenge kept me going while I struggled with my existence for centuries. I knew I needed to accept the darkest parts of myself to succeed. And yet, revenge wouldn't change a thing about what I was. I was stuck living a life I despised.

"But what you are doesn't determine your life. Your decisions do. Vampirism gives you the power to control your fate. It's not the cause of your suffering. Bad people brought you down, but their deeds don't define you. Being a vampire doesn't make you a monster. Like humans, vampires can be good or bad. Some of us didn't choose this life, but we can choose our fate thanks to the power they forced upon us."

"What a speech. Do you believe in your words?"

"Yes." The corners of his lips curled into a smile as he stared into the distance. "Although it took me four centuries and meeting Lilah to come to terms with what I am. You're lucky. There is already someone by your side who sees you for who you truly are."

Someone by my side? Her heart rocketed in her chest. "Are you talking about Dave?"

"Obviously, yes. You changed his beliefs and the way he looks at vampires. Now you need to learn how to see yourself through his eyes."

Had she changed Dave's outlook on vampires? Soon after they'd met, he told her they could never be friends. And now? They were more than friends. He trusted her with his life.

"You've done a lot for him and the other hunters, haven't you?" Cain asked.

She nodded.

"Those deeds define you. Being a vampire enables you to fight for them. Your power is a good thing."

"What if I lose control and the darkness takes over?" She swallowed. "What if I hurt someone I care about?"

"Don't underestimate yourself. Besides, we're here to help. I'll make sure you don't do anything you'd regret."

She didn't trust him with the lives of those she cared about. But in this moment, they were in the middle of a deep forest with no humans around for her to hurt.

"Okay," she said, "I'll give it a shot."

"Good girl. Let's try a meditation technique. Sit down and concentrate on your power. Picture it as something good, something invigorating. Don't try to contain it. Let it flow freely through your body."

She flopped onto the ground and closed her eyes. In her mind, she replaced the image of her power as something dark and dangerous with an empowering light, helping her to overcome any obstacle. A pleasantly warm feeling spread through her body.

"Very good." Cain's voice interrupted her peaceful meditation. "Now, attack me."

She leaped to her feet and charged at him with raised fists. Her saber still lay on the ground, but she didn't need it with the power flowing through her. She longed to feel the impact of her punches and kicks.

Cain still blocked her attacks, but he retreated a few steps.

"Much better. Now that's something I can work with," he said before fighting back with more force.

****

Dave watched as Sarah vanished into the forest. Then he turned his attention to Lilah. The young woman was taller and less delicate than Sarah.

She watched him with a calculating smile. "So, how do you want to do this?"

"Do what exactly?"

"Drink blood? Straight from the vein, or do you prefer to mix it with a drink?"

He wrinkled his nose. "It sounds gross either way, so let's just get it over with."

"Okay. I hope your girlfriend won't get jealous about you drinking my blood."

"We're not in such a relationship."

"If you say so." With a chuckle, she bit into her wrist and offered him her blood.

Slowly, he bent down and sucked on the bleeding wound. His body recoiled at the metallic taste, yet he forced himself to gulp down every drop until the bite closed on its own.

When he pulled away, his body vibrated with energy.

Despite the late hour, his eyes could make out his

surroundings better, and the swoosh of the wind in the trees sounded louder than before. He took a deep breath and marveled at the mix of olfactory sensations flashing through his mind. The scent of the trees and shrubs around them invigorated him, and he could faintly smell Sarah even though she'd left. Her lovely fragrance put a smile on his lips.

"You're quite observant," she said. "Back when I drank blood for the first time, I didn't notice these changes in my perception."

"How did you…?"

"I can read your mind. Don't worry about it." She smiled cheekily. "I'll teach you how to shut me out later on. For now, let's fight. I'm curious what you're capable of."

Chapter 24

The rising sun colored the edge of the horizon red when Sarah returned with Cain to the cabin after several hours of training. Inside, she found herself in a rustic living room comprising two dark leather couches with white fur pillows, a wooden table, and a fireplace. A wolfskin rug decorated the floor in front of it. A simplistic kitchen in the room's corner offered a fridge, a stove, a sink, and a countertop. In the opposite corner, a spiral staircase with wooden steps led upstairs.

Dave lay slumped on one couch with a cup of coffee in his hand, while Lilah lounged on the other one.

"I'll take a shower and then retire for the night. See you tomorrow." Cain headed upstairs.

Sarah nodded absentmindedly and sagged onto Dave's couch. "How was your training?"

"Challenging. We spent most of the night fighting. Lilah's blood allowed me to keep up with her training. The effect truly astonished me. I'm still pretty tired, so I'll retire soon as well. I only stayed up to see how you were doing."

She clenched her teeth as the thought of Dave consuming Lilah's blood sent a burning sensation through her chest. "I'm tired as well. During the training, I tapped into more power than ever before, which was frightening. If I learn to control it, I'll be stronger than ever."

"Speaking of tired, this cabin only has two bedrooms, so you two need to share," Lilah said.

She shrugged. "We've shared hotel rooms before."

"Also, there's only one king-sized bed." Lilah smirked. "Speaking of beds, I'll join Cain upstairs. Good night."

"I could sleep down here as well," she offered once Lilah had left them alone.

He shook his head. "A king-sized bed is big enough to fit the two of us. As long as you don't mind sharing with me?"

Sleeping in the same bed wasn't much different from spending the night in the same hotel room, right? So why did her stomach quiver? No matter what Lilah or anyone else implied, they were merely friends. Since she was a vampire, nothing could ever happen between them, anyway. And by now, she handled her hunger well enough to stay near him, so there was no logical reason to refuse. "Okay."

"Well then, I'll go to bed. Good night." He yawned and got up.

She followed him upstairs and headed for the shower. After freshening up and putting on a nightgown from her overnight bag, she entered the bedroom. Apart from the spacious bed with red sheets, the room comprised two wooden bedside tables and a sliding door wardrobe with a mirror front. A huge painting of a snowy landscape with trees and mountains hung on the wall.

Dave was already asleep, breathing evenly. Careful not to wake him, she settled down next to him.

Despite her exhaustion from training, she lay awake for a while. As she watched the man sleeping next to her, the strange longing to cuddle up to him and hold him close emerged. Yet she dismissed it like so many times before. She was an abomination and not meant for a life with him.

****

Hunger woke Sarah after a few hours of sleep. With the previous night's training, its intensity didn't surprise her. She dreaded the idea of hunting for blood. Yet her cravings would only grow and become harder to control if she waited. Thus, she got up, put on a tracksuit, and headed downstairs.

Lilah greeted her from the couch. "Hey, I've been waiting for you. Ready to go hunting?"

"I'd rather hunt for vampires than for blood."

Lilah shrugged. "Suit yourself. I need to feed now. If you don't want to join me, you're on your own later on."

"My body is longing for blood," she admitted, biting her lip.

"Then come." Lilah grinned, offering her hand.

Could a young vampire like Lilah help her if she lost control while feeding?

"Wouldn't it be…safer if Cain joined us as well?" she asked.

Lilah scoffed. "Just because I'm young doesn't mean I can't handle myself around blood. In fact, I'm the better choice for helping you control your urges."

"Why?"

"You'll see. I promise you and whomever you choose for your meal will be fine."

Reluctantly, she grasped the female vampire's hand. Moments later, they stood in an alley in a dark, run-down neighborhood. With no streetlamps in sight, the only light stemmed from the partially clouded moon. An older man staggered at the opposite end of the alley, presumably on his way home after having too much to drink.

"Mind if I go first?" Lilah asked.

She shook her head and watched as Lilah took a deep breath before catching up to the man and grabbing him from behind. She buried her teeth in his throat before he could even cry out. After a couple of seconds, his heartbeat evened out as if he'd fallen asleep.

She couldn't keep her eyes off the feeding vampire. When she inhaled the scent of fresh blood, her stomach rumbled. A wave of euphoria washed through her as she imagined sinking her fangs into his throat as well.

She gritted her teeth when the beast in her roared and demanded a taste. Blood dominated her thoughts. Soon, she lost all sense of what was happening around her.

After what felt like hours, Lilah shook her, snapping her out of her trance. "Focus. You're already lost in the blood before you've even tasted it."

When she looked around, the victim lay on the ground with his back against a wall, snoring loudly.

"Sorry," she said. "Will he be all right?"

"Don't worry about him. He'll wake up in a few minutes thinking he fell asleep from his drunkenness. Now come on, we need to find your meal."

She followed Lilah to a park, where a young woman in a black goth outfit loafed on a bench and smoked. A single streetlamp bathed her in a faint, yellow light.

"She's young enough to handle a little blood loss, even if you end up taking a bit too much," Lilah said.

Her heart romped in her chest at the promise of fresh blood. Could she handle it?

"Stop thinking so much. Clear your head. Concentrate on yourself and your emotions. Once you feel you're in control, go for her."

She nodded slowly, taking deep breaths to calm her mind. After a couple of minutes, she approached the woman from behind, grabbed her, and sank her teeth into her flesh. The taste of the warm, sweet blood trumped everything she'd imagined. Nothing had ever tasted so rich and exhilarating. She was bathing in a sea of euphoria. Nothing else mattered anymore. Why had she insisted on blood bags for so long?

A weird clicking sound brought her back to reality, and Lilah's voice entered her subconscious. *You're hurting her. Focus. And ease her suffering.*

A shudder ran through her when she noticed the girl's whimpering and the trashing of her heart.

She pictured the girl falling asleep on the bench and planted the memory of having a nightmare in her mind. The girl calmed down, and Sarah concentrated on the delicious taste again.

Another sound pulled her focus back to Lilah, who told her to stop. She remembered the difficulty of releasing a victim, but to her surprise, it was much easier this time. She closed the bite marks with her own blood before laying the woman down on the bench.

"Good job." Lilah smiled.

"How did you...?" She frowned. What had Lilah done? She wouldn't have been able to handle the rush of feeding on her own, so how could Lilah give her the control she lacked?

"I know a thing or two about controlling, or rather fooling, minds," Lilah answered. "Don't worry about it. You'll be able to handle yourself in no time. You've starved yourself for too long, so it'll take time to get used to the allure of blood."

"Thank you," Sarah mumbled.

She didn't want to trust these vampires, but they made it hard not to. Without Lilah's help, she might have killed the woman.

Chapter 25

Disappointment welled up in Dave when he opened his eyes and found himself alone in the bed. Had Sarah taken the couch after all? He shook the thought from his mind, stretched, and got up. After a quick shower, he checked downstairs.

Cain was reading a book in the living room. He glanced up when Dave approached him. "Lilah and Sarah are hunting for a meal. You're stuck training with me tonight."

Dave nodded and raided the fridge for some breakfast. "Give me a few minutes to eat and then we can get started."

After a cup of instant coffee, a slice of bread, and two granola bars, he fetched his sword and headed outside.

Cain had him drink a few sips of his blood before chasing him through the forest for two hours as a warm-up exercise.

Eventually, exhaustion overcame him. He stopped running and hid behind a large tree, gasping for air.

Out of nowhere, Cain appeared in front of him. "Why do humans always think hiding from a vampire is a good idea when they're supposed to run?"

"Because running is exhausting for us."

"A vampire will always find you, though. Your beating heart will lead him right to you."

"Well, sorry for being alive," he said wryly.

Cain chuckled. "Lilah did the same thing the first time I ran with her." Then his expression became thoughtful. "I don't know how you do it."

"Do what?"

"Remain by her side, feeling the way you do, without being in a relationship."

Dave frowned at the sudden change of topic. "I'm happy simply being near her. She's been through so much…I aim to give her the comfort she needs without pressuring her into anything."

"You're both fools. She has feelings for you, too, although she doesn't know what they mean. She'll never commit to a relationship with you—a human—without a nudge. After all, she considers herself not worthy of love because she's a monster."

He sucked in a breath, and his heart rollicked. If she truly felt the same, he would no longer repress his feelings. "Why are you telling me this?"

"You're good for her. She needs someone who believes in her and heals the scars of her past. Love can elevate you to new heights. Anyway"—Cain drew his weapon—"enough talking. It's time for some sword practice."

****

When Lilah teleported them back to the cabin, Cain and Dave were training. Their swords clashed in the distance, disturbing the silence of the surrounding woods.

"Guess you're training with me tonight," Lilah said.

Sarah curled her lips into a grimace. She'd barely talked to or spent time with Dave since arriving at the cabin.

"Your own fault for not making the most of your time in bed together." Lilah winked at her.

She growled. "We're friends."

"Stop fooling yourself. Be thankful you've already found someone precious to you. Others search for decades or even centuries until they find the one. Why do you keep him at a distance?"

"It's none of your business."

"It is if you constantly think about him instead of our training." Lilah sighed. "Why are you afraid of letting him get close? Your thoughts reveal the truth— you're both in love with each other."

Her heart rocketed in her chest at Lilah's assessment, yet she ignored it. "He's my closest friend, so why should I mess our friendship up by asking for something I shouldn't have? Humans and vampires should not be together."

"Bullshit. You'll mess everything up by doing nothing. How long do you think he'll be content just staying by your side? If you risk nothing, you'll eventually lose everything."

"What do you know about risks? You already got everything you want, don't you?"

"How do you think I reached this point? I've risked my life more than once and challenged countless vampires on my journey to become one. I even fought Cain in a battle for my life. If you really want something, commit to it, and do everything in your power to achieve your goal—whether it's love or revenge."

Was there more to Lilah than her arrogant and carefree attitude had let her believe? "Do relationships between humans and vampires even work?"

"Of course. And sex can be quite rewarding for both,

especially if you inject him with the right fluid."

Heat crept up her cheeks. "Too much information."

Lilah shrugged. "Drinking blood can be very erotic if you know how and where to bite."

"Let's start with the training, shall we?" Time to change the topic.

"Fine with me. Wait here." Lilah vanished, only to return with headphones and a blindfold.

"What…?"

"You rely on your human senses too much instead of using your vampiric instincts. So tonight, you'll fight me without sight or hearing."

"How am I supposed to fight without my senses?" She frowned.

"Don't think too much about it. I underwent the same training as a human, so I'm sure you'll manage."

She'd ignored her instincts so far because they were part of the beast in her. Was it safe to release it?

Lilah rolled her eyes. "There is no beast. Your heightened emotions take control sometimes, but they're part of who you are. If you accept them, you'll eventually learn to control them."

Every fiber of her being rebelled against accepting Lilah's assertion, but…based on the previous night's training success, Lilah and Cain seemed to know what they were talking about. So, she gritted her teeth, covered her eyes, and put on the headphones.

After overcoming her disorientation, she focused on the power emanating from her opponent. Yet it revealed nothing about Lilah's movements. When the vampire kicked her, she doubled over in pain.

Two punches later, she crouched on the floor. Lilah wanted her to release her inner beast? *Fine.* With a growl, she let her power loose. Instead of focusing on her surroundings, she only concentrated on herself and the flow of energy through her body.

When the urge to move overcame her, she jumped, spun around, and kicked straight ahead. Her foot collided with something hard in front of her.

Very good, Lilah's voice echoed in her head. *Now keep it up.*

Listening to her instincts, she sparred with Lilah for hours. The longer they fought, the more natural the energy felt within her.

****

After practicing his sword skills for most of the night, Dave settled on the couch with a cup of coffee, nibbling on a pepperoni pizza Cain had picked up for him in a nearby town. Sarah was still training with Lilah. Did she truly reciprocate his feelings? If her prejudice against herself was the only obstacle between them, he'd tear it down and make her his. They were great together, and being a different species was no reason not to date her. Of course, convincing her would be the real challenge.

His stomach fluttered when the two women entered the cabin an hour later. Lilah exchanged a glance with Cain, and the couple vanished upstairs.

"Can we talk?" he asked.

"Um, sure." Sarah plummeted onto the couch next to him. "About what?"

He shifted on the couch to face her. "Us."

"What do you mean?" Her voice sounded higher than usual.

"For the past year, we've spent almost every night together—training or hunting vampires. Having you by my side feels natural. Still, you've always kept a distance, making me believe you preferred it this way. Through conversations with our two…allies here, I've realized you suppress your true feelings because you believe they're wrong."

He watched her intently. She stared at the floor, a mix of emotions flashing over her face.

Then she looked up. "You shouldn't believe anything these vampires tell you."

"Why would they lie about this? And even if they did, it doesn't change my feelings. I'm content just being by your side if that's all you long for. But if even a part of you hopes for something more, I can't stay quiet any longer."

With a sigh, she met his gaze. "You're forgetting I'm a monster."

"I don't see a monster when I look at you." His voice broke with sadness. How could she still talk about herself this way?

"It doesn't matter. Vampires and humans can't coexist. Any relationship is doomed before it even starts."

"I don't believe that." He framed her face with his hands. "Being a vampire doesn't condemn you to a life of solitude and suffering. You deserve much more."

She shivered and closed her eyes, as if battling her inner demons.

With a quaking heart, he leaned forward and tentatively pressed his lips to hers. Her body froze for a second before she responded to the kiss.

Her soft lips parted slightly, inviting him in. Encouraged by her reaction, he deepened the kiss. But when their tongues met, she pulled away.

She gaped at him. Then she bolted through the front door.

Chapter 26

Sarah fled the cabin to clear her head, running aimlessly through the woods. Tears streamed down her face. Why was she crying? And what was she running from? Dave? Or her feelings?

Eventually, she dropped onto the forest floor and looked up at the twinkling stars. She'd run from her first kiss like an idiot. Or had she been an idiot for reveling in the sensation in the first place, even if only for a second? Why had fate put her on this path to despair?

When the black sky turned blue and the stars vanished, a twig snapped, and footsteps rustled the leaves on the forest floor. Lilah appeared in her peripheral vision. "Why do you close yourself off from any possibility of happiness?"

She gulped. "Dave and I, we live in two different worlds."

"No, you don't. So far, you've only encountered poor examples, but there are many more vampires out there. Let me show you how well we can coexist with humans." Lilah held out her hand, waiting.

What did she have to lose? After wiping any remaining tears from her face, she got up and clasped her hand.

The familiar sensation of dropping didn't last long. Moments later, they found themselves in a cramped apartment, or rather, a house trailer. Sunrays gleamed through the window, revealing they'd traveled at least a few time zones east.

"A friend of mine lives here, but she's working now. With luck, you'll get to see her in action. Follow me." Lilah opened the door and hopped outside.

A multitude of foreign voices and smells greeted Sarah as she followed her to a gigantic, yellow-and-red-striped tent. "What is this?"

"Have you never seen a circus?" Lilah tilted her head.

She shook hers. "Visiting a circus wasn't on my kidnappers' agenda."

"Let's watch the show then. You'll love it!" Lilah's eyes sparkled as she grabbed Sarah's hand, dragged her to the entrance, and bought two tickets for the late afternoon performance.

They sat in the heart of the tent, right in front of the circular stage. The surrounding seats filled quickly, and the otherwise human audience chatted excitedly. The anticipation was almost tangible, a hum of energy filling the air.

Sarah gasped when a dark-haired woman in a glittering suit—the circus director—entered the stage to greet the audience. Her supernatural aura revealed her as a vampire. Yet she paid no special attention to Sarah and smiled as if speaking in front of hundreds of humans was the most natural occurrence.

After the director left, a petite woman entered the stage and headed for two strips of fabric hanging from the ceiling. She climbed up and wrapped her left leg in the silk. Letting herself fall head first, she spun around in a circle, with only the fabric on her thigh holding her. When she spotted them, her mouth opened in surprise before a smile formed on her lips.

"She's a good friend of mine," Lilah whispered.

"But…she's human."

Lilah chuckled. "So?"

She could not avert her eyes as the acrobat untangled herself to climb even higher and strike different poses with the fabric, wrapping and unwrapping various parts of her body. Every movement seemed perfect. How could a human move so elegantly, fast, and controlled?

The following acts were no less breathtaking. After the curtain fell, Lilah told her the director had trained with the humans and helped them reach their potential. They had no clue as to her true nature.

Once they left the circus tent, the acrobat from the opening performance ran up to Lilah and pulled her into a long hug. "Lilah, you're here! I've missed you."

"Hi, Vanessa. Sorry, it's been a while." She gestured toward Sarah. "And I've brought a friend. Today was her first time visiting a circus."

Vanessa turned to her, tilting her head. "Your first? Ever? How did you like it?"

"Oh, it was…um…wow. Just amazing."

"Glad you enjoyed it." Vanessa beamed at them. "Anyway, I've got to prepare for the evening show. Sophie said you could meet her in her trailer."

"Great, thank you," Lilah said. "Good luck with your upcoming performance!"

When Vanessa vanished into the tent, Lilah led her back to the trailer they'd arrived in earlier. Inside, the other vampire rested on a small beige couch, her arms folded behind her head.

"Hi Lexi, how are you?" Lilah asked.

"Lexi? Didn't the woman say her name was

Sophie?" Sarah frowned.

"Hello." Lexi slash Sophie laughed, got up, and hugged Lilah. "Both names are fine. If a 'Lexi' owned this circus for over two centuries, people would ask dangerous questions. So, I reinvent myself every two decades. But enough about me. Who are you?"

"Sarah."

When she held out her hand, Lexi pulled her into a hug. She stiffened, but forced herself not to pull back.

"Nice to meet you. So, what brings you two here?"

"Sarah doesn't believe in a peaceful coexistence of vampires and humans," said Lilah. "So, I brought her here to show her a successful counterexample."

Lexi eyed her from head to toe. "You've only crossed paths with the wrong kind of vampires so far, haven't you? Don't let those terrible examples stain your perception of what you are. We've got the power to do great things if we put our mind to it. And humans can be a part of our lives, too. Together, we create beautiful things."

"What do you do when your employees or the audience get suspicious?" She narrowed her eyes.

"Are you insinuating I'd kill them to protect my identity?"

"I..."

"Don't fret." Lexi smiled. "They're my family. I could never hurt them. If someone suspects my identity, I usually fake my death or vanish for some other reason. Two or three years later, I return as a daughter, cousin, or other relative. People want to believe lies if they explain the impossible, like someone never aging."

"Huh."

"I hope this opens your eyes to a new perspective.

Unfortunately, I need to go backstage now. The next performance starts in twenty minutes. If you don't plan to watch or join in on the performance, why don't we meet up again another night?"

"Oh, I won't perform tonight. We'll get going." Lilah hugged the other vampire goodbye. "See you soon, and thanks for your time."

****

After another teleportation, they arrived in an alley in the middle of a business district. Lilah led Sarah into a gigantic building with a glass front. They took an elevator to the top floor.

The doors opened into an office reception area, where an older woman with short, brown hair in a black skirt suit greeted them. "Good evening. What can I do for you two ladies?"

"Hello, remember me?" Lilah smiled at the woman. "I'm…Laurant's cousin from abroad. I'm in town for a layover. Is he in tonight?"

"Of course, Lilah, wasn't it? He's in his office. Do you want me to announce you?"

"No need. I'll surprise him. His office was down the hall, right?"

When the woman nodded, Lilah strode past her, through a long corridor, and to an office behind a glass door. Sarah followed her to find a young man with blond hair in a fancy business suit inside. He almost felt human. Only a barely perceptible aura of supernatural energy surrounded him.

"Lilah." He rose from his large leather chair and bowed to her.

"Stop with the formalities." Lilah rolled her eyes. "Based on your age and everything you taught me, you should definitely not be the one bowing."

An amused smile spread across his lips. "Fair enough. To what do I owe the pleasure?"

"I wanted my friend Sarah here to witness how we thrive among humans."

Laurant walked past his large glass table and offered her his hand. "Pleasure to meet you. My name is Laurant."

"Likewise." She shook his hand. "So, you work here?"

"It's my company. I founded it eight years ago. Technology and data are still all the rage."

"You've always been fascinated by mankind's newest inventions, haven't you? With all these gadgets here, you can't even deny it." Lilah pointed at several showcases decorating the room. They contained different mechanical devices, drawings, and old books. Most of the items looked like they belonged in a museum instead of an office.

"True," Laurant said. "It's a big part of the zeitgeist and helps me stay connected."

"Do your employees know about you?" Sarah asked.

"No. They simply take me for an eccentric collector of old artifacts. I don't hire anyone for more than a couple of years. And I never feed from my employees or business contacts. Well, almost never. The exception proves the rule."

"But you're not really close to any of them, are you?"

His expression turned into a pensive smile. "There are rare exceptions. I'm seeing a human right now."

"You are? Why haven't you told me about her?"

Lilah pouted.

"You've got enough on your plate. Besides, this is brand new. Tonight will be our second date."

"Oh wow. Then we won't keep you much longer," Lilah said. "One more question, though. Will you be at the fight club one of these nights?"

"Probably not. If you're looking for some fun, the regulars will be there tomorrow."

"We'll think about it. Thank you. And enjoy your date." Lilah grinned and headed outside.

She followed her out of the building and into a dark alley, from where they returned to the cabin.

****

The bright midday sun greeted them, prickling on Sarah's skin. A few animals scurried through the woods, and a woodpecker hammered nearby.

"I hope meeting my friends gave you some food for thought. Yes, vampires can be cruel and vindictive. Most simply wish to live their lives. Among humans. You and Dave *can* work out." Lilah yawned. "And I need sleep. See you tomorrow."

They both headed inside and up the stairs.

After a quick shower, Sarah tiptoed into the room she shared with Dave. When her eyes landed on his sleeping form, the urge to cuddle up to him welled up in her again. This time, she didn't fight it.

Chapter 27

A soft, warm body nestled against Dave's chest. He blinked his eyes open and moaned slightly. She'd come back. If this was a dream, he never wanted to wake up. And if it wasn't…His heart fluttered as he pulled her into a tighter embrace.

They lay like this for at least an hour until she stirred in his arms. Sleepy eyes looked up at him through tousled hair.

"Good morning." He smiled at her.

"Morning." Her cheeks turned rosy. "I…"

"You've returned."

She nibbled on her lip. "I'm not sure how any of this relationship stuff works, or if it can work at all between us. If you truly want this, I'm willing to give us a chance, though."

A pleasant, stimulating heat filled his body, and he placed a kiss on her temple. "I do. And I've never dated a vampire either, so let's take it slowly and learn how to make this work along the way."

"Okay." She sighed. "I need to get up and feed, though."

He tightened his hold on her. "I'm not ready to let you out of my arms yet."

"But…" Her lips parted slightly as she gazed at him.

He brushed her bottom lip with his thumb. A pinprick of pain pierced his finger when he deliberately cut it on her fang.

She shuddered as he smeared the building drop of blood on her lips. "What are you doing?"

"I can't bear the thought of you touching another man right now. So, drink my blood instead."

She stiffened. "I only started feeding on humans again last night. It's not safe."

"I trust in you. Besides, Lilah and Cain are probably listening to our every word. They could stop you if you went too far."

"Are you sure?" Her eyes searched his.

"Very." He'd fantasized about it too many times...

Slowly, she moved her mouth closer to his throat, and he lifted his chin to give her better access. Her breath tickled the shell of his ear as her breathing sped up. He shivered when her soft lips touched his neck, kissing him at first. She licked and nibbled teasingly on his skin before piercing it with her fangs.

Instead of pain, a blazing fire of passion, unlike anything he knew, flooded his senses.

More. The single thought penetrated his mind, and he pressed her body even closer to his. Nothing mattered except for the feeling of holding her in his arms and this incredible heat pulsating through his body. For all he cared, she could suck him dry.

His head spun from the rush of endorphins and losing blood. Her bite gave him the most exquisite high—he was floating through space and dancing on clouds.

It ended much too soon. He was vaguely aware of the sound of a door closing right after she released him.

She looked at him with wide eyes. "Are you all right?"

"Of course, beautiful. Why did you stop?" He stilled at the weak sound of his voice.

"Because I already drank too much." After biting into her wrist, she held it to his mouth. "Here, this will strengthen you."

He gulped down her blood without hesitation, ignoring the nauseating taste.

Once her wound closed, she pulled away. "This was a mistake."

"No." He grabbed her top, his fingers tangling in the fabric to keep her close. "You took a bit too much? So what? I can handle it. No more running from this."

Her eyes widened when he pulled her even closer, putting one hand on her waist and the other on the back of her head. When her lips parted, his mouth crashed down on hers.

Despite the residual taste of his blood in her mouth, he relished her intoxicating flavor. Her tongue played with his—carefully at first and then more and more demanding.

They both panted when he broke free to catch his breath. Her aquamarine-blue eyes sparkled like crystals as he stared into them.

"Everything okay?" he asked.

She answered him with the sweetest smile. "Yes."

Suppressing his desire to explore her whole body next, he pressed another kiss to her cute nose and snuggled against her. After all, they'd agreed on taking things slowly. And he hadn't even taken her on a proper date.

A knock sounded on the door, and Lilah entered with a smug grin. "I'll take you to the fight club tonight for some combat practice. With the time difference, we won't leave before morning. Make the most of your time until then."

Sarah's head turned red.

Dave glared at Lilah. "Thanks for the information. Please *leave*."

"See you in a few hours." With a chuckle, she left them alone.

Chapter 28

Distant yelling sounded from within a shabby warehouse in an otherwise quiet industrial area. The building also hummed with supernatural energy, making Sarah wish she'd packed her saber despite Lilah's insistence on weaponless fighting.

She and Dave followed her through a side entrance into the warehouse, passing several rooms filled with papers, cardboard boxes, and other discarded items. When they approached the only dimly lit room in the building, the noise hushed down.

Around a dozen vampires, most of them dressed like punks or goths, kneeled down when Lilah set foot in the room. Without even glancing at them, she strutted to a wooden box and enthroned herself on it.

"Get up," she said.

The vampires obeyed, looking at her expectantly. Who was she *really* to provoke such a reaction and obedience?

She gestured toward Sarah and Dave, who were still waiting at the entrance. "You'll fight my two friends tonight. One-on-one, like always. No killing allowed. If one of you successfully brings down both of them, I'll owe you a favor."

The vampires whispered among themselves.

One of them stepped forward with a quick bow of his head. He was a punk with a messy green mullet. "I'd like to go first."

"Very well," Lilah said. "Sarah, do you want to begin?"

She nodded and stepped into the center of the large room to join the contender.

"To a fair fight." He inclined his head in greeting.

Gritting her teeth, she nodded. As if vampires ever fought fair.

Lilah counted down, "Three…two…one…Go."

Sarah balled her fist and struck first. The punk blocked her with one hand while punching back with the other. He ducked when she tried again. They exchanged several blows, neither of them landing any deciding hits.

"You're supposed to tap into your power and use your instincts," Lilah chided her from the sidelines. "Even if you think you don't need them against him."

She growled, hating the idea of tapping into her darkness with Dave so close by and surrounded by so many beasts. But that was the whole point of this exercise, wasn't it?

Exhaling loudly, she relinquished control and allowed her power to flow through her. When the punk charged at her, her body almost acted on its own. She ducked, turned, and attacked with a spinning back heel kick, sending her opponent flying.

He crashed into a wooden box. Groaning, he got back to his feet and cracked his knuckles. "Not bad."

With deliberate, slow steps, he circled her. She let him, closing her eyes and concentrating only on herself. When he kicked at her from behind, she spun around in time to block his leg with hers.

He jumped back, building up speed before charging toward her again with more force. Crossing her arms in front of her chest, she blocked and kicked him in the stomach at the same time.

He doubled over and sank to the ground.

"Are you done?" she asked.

"Yeah," he grunted, "I surrender."

The vampires surrounding them clapped, causing her expression to contort into a frown. Rubbing the back of her neck, she took them in more closely. Despite their rough appearance, she saw respect instead of menace in their eyes.

"Next one is up against Dave," Lilah announced. "Who wants to fight him? Oh, and don't underestimate him because of his humanity."

A chubby, bald-headed vampire volunteered. With a bow toward Lilah, he said, "I've learned not to underestimate humans."

When Dave stepped up to face him, Sarah retreated to the side of the room.

Like before, Lilah counted down to the start of the match. As soon as the "Go" left her lips, the vampire stormed at Dave, punching him in the guts before he could defend himself. With a gasp, he doubled over, clutching his arms to his stomach.

She sucked in a breath.

When the vampire kept pounding on Dave, she snarled. A wave of energy rushed through her, waiting to be released. How dare he hurt Dave?

"Don't interfere," Lilah's tense voice cautioned her. "This is a safe space to test his limits. He can surrender if it gets too much."

Growling, she balled her fists so tight it hurt. Dave had to face this enemy alone. After all, if he didn't succeed here, how could she risk letting him face the royal family? Yet with every punch he took, her pulse sped up.

"Enough. My turn now." He groaned after blocking the bald vampire's fist. Pushing him back with surprising force, Dave caused the vampire to stumble.

Before his opponent regained balance, he kicked his shins from behind to make him fall.

When the vampire landed on his back, Dave jumped on top of him. With one knee above his heart, the other constricting his throat, and his hands fixing the vampire's arms, Dave didn't leave him any wiggle room.

"I think we have a winner," Lilah announced.

Unable to speak, the vampire grunted. The others applauded again.

Sarah and Dave took turns defeating one vampire after the other. Just as he defeated the last opponent, Laurant appeared in the doorway, wearing an even fancier suit than the night before. Its light blue color contrasted with the dark outfits of the other vampires.

"Welcome," Lilah greeted him from atop the box. "I thought you couldn't make it. What changed your mind?"

He shrugged. "You know me. I can't resist a good brawl."

"True. Sorry for taking up your spot."

"I'm not here to watch." His eyes wandered to Sarah and then Dave, who still panted from his last encounter. "How about another match—you two against me?"

"Together?" She raised an eyebrow. The energy in his aura didn't impress her.

"Yes. And why don't you heal your friend with a little blood before we get started? His previous fights obviously took their toll."

With a shake of the head, she gave Dave a few sips of her blood. Was the vampire's arrogance based on stupidity or hidden power? He even offered to let them attack first.

She exchanged a glance with Dave. Together, they charged at him from two sides.

Laurant sidestepped them so fast she had to spin around to avoid crashing into Dave.

"Again," he baited them.

This time, she let Dave attack first before kicking at Laurant. The vampire evaded Dave's punch, grabbed her leg, and hurtled her against Dave. They both landed in a cardboard box. Maybe his skill justified his arrogance.

"Let me attack and wait for an opening," she instructed Dave.

With a nod, he fell back, giving her space. Without him at risk, she let her instincts take over.

She struck at Laurant with lightning speed. Feigning an attack from the right, she jumped at the last moment, swirled, and kicked at his head from above. He blocked with his arm, pushing her back through the air.

The moment she landed on the ground, Dave took her place, punching Laurant's back several times. The vampire brushed it off like the touch of a feather. His counterattack sent Dave flying into another box.

She came at him again. No matter how much force she used, Laurant met her blows with the same vigor. He didn't even bother fending off most of her hits. Instead, he used her proximity to strike back twice as hard.

They kept fighting—Sarah and Dave taking turns whenever Laurant pushed one of them back—until Dave collapsed, too exhausted to get up again. Desperate to end the fight, she focused all her energy on a final punch to his gut.

Laurant doubled over. Then his smile widened. "Now, *that* was fun."

With a roundhouse kick, he knocked her away.

She crashed into the wall and relented. Everything hurt, and she'd used up too much energy. "I surrender."

"Good job, you two." Lilah jumped off the box to help Dave up.

"But we lost." He groaned.

"Doesn't matter. I didn't expect you to win against him."

"You actually hurt me." Laurant offered his hand to help Sarah up. "Few people can claim the same."

She ignored the hand and pushed to her feet. "Doesn't feel like an accomplishment to me."

Lilah grinned. "Well, then you need to train harder."

Chapter 29

Dressed in a black suit with a light blue shirt, Dave led Sarah through the street with his arm around her waist. Her breathtaking black dress emphasized her feminine figure. It was sleeveless, and the hem ended a few inches below her ass, giving her flexibility while hiding the important things. If only they were on the way to a fancy event, for example, a ballet performance. He'd buy her a bouquet of red roses and treat her to the most unforgettable date—she only deserved the best. Unfortunately, they'd planned a different agenda for the night. His weapons hung from his belt, while she had her saber strapped to her back.

Lilah and Cain were following them in a similar getup—he was wearing a black suit with a white shirt while she'd combined a long-sleeved, almost transparent, black blouse with black dress pants. They'd insisted on the fancy getup to blend in at their target location.

With dawn looming on the horizon, only a few humans would be around, and most vampires had left for their homes, which made this the perfect time to infiltrate without causing too much of a scene.

Sarah craned her neck to look up at the shimmering front of the tall, fully illuminated building. "What a bold choice of venue for their headquarters."

If anyone else had told him vampire royalty

occupied this futuristic skyscraper in downtown Seattle, he'd have laughed. But even if he didn't trust Cain's intel—and after a fortnight of training with him and Lilah, he had little reason not to—the cluster of supernatural energy on the top floors served as a dead giveaway.

"Their boldness is one of many reasons we need to eradicate them. Let's go. There is a hidden entrance over there." Cain led them to a passage at the side of the building.

Turning the corner, they found a section of wall devoid of doors or windows.

"How are we supposed to—" Dave asked when a *beep* sounded next to him.

A crack in the otherwise flat surface of the wall—an inconspicuous door—opened and revealed a young woman in a red dress. A surprised "Oh" escaped her before she narrowed her eyes on Sarah and the other two vampires. "Who are you? What are you doing here?"

Giving the woman no time to act, Lilah pounced, grabbed her by the arm, and pulled her outside.

"Don't kill her," Sarah hissed. "She's human."

"I know." Lilah growled. She pressed the woman against the wall, forcing her to look into her eyes. "Stay quiet. Don't fight."

Once the woman relaxed, Lilah bit into her throat. As soon as the woman slumped in her arms, she laid her on the ground. "They only put a handful of human guards with assault rifles on the lower levels. How cocky and foolish."

"Did you pick up on that by reading her thoughts?" Dave asked. Her abilities scared and amazed him at the same time. Would Sarah have possessed the same powers if she'd embraced all of herself earlier? He quickly dismissed the thought—she was perfect the way she was.

"Not exactly. She actually had a mental guard up, which is why I fed on her to draw the images from her blood." Lilah fished for something in the woman's clothes and pulled out an ID card. "This should open a few doors for us."

To illustrate her point, she opened the hidden door, which had slid shut again at some point, by holding the card to a blinking spot on the wall next to the crack.

They sneaked inside and found themselves in a windowless corridor, illuminated by fluorescent light. They followed it for a while until they arrived at a junction. A sign on the wall informed them the pantry was to the right and down the stairs, whereas the left path led to the elevators. Lilah and Cain turned left without hesitation.

What did vampires store in a pantry? His skin crawled as he considered the question. "What if there are human captives down there?"

"Oh, there most definitely are," Lilah said. "We can't afford to rescue anyone until we've eliminated all vampires, though."

Sarah looked back and forth between the two vampires to her left and the stairs to her right.

"They're right." He clenched his jaws and followed them. "Don't forget why we're here."

As they rounded the corner, the corridor opened up to reveal a grand hall with a gleaming marble floor and several tall pillars stretching up to the ceiling. A lone guard with a rifle leaned against the wall next to two elevators. Cain charged at him and snapped his neck before he could even react to their presence.

His stomach twisted at the sight of the body.

"How dare you kill him?" Sarah hissed.

"Every human with a weapon knows exactly what they're protecting here," Lilah said. "Trust me, this ruthless bastard had it coming."

"If you can't handle it, turn around," Cain added.

Sarah balled her fists next to him. "No, I'm good."

"Me, too." He'd stay by her side at all costs.

With a swipe of the ID card, they entered the elevator. The control panel had buttons from one to thirteen, with a key symbol next to the top three floors.

"Let's see how high we can get with this." Lilah held the ID card to a scanner embedded in the control panel. Starting at the top, she pressed one button after another until finally one of them worked and a bright red "11" glowed on the display. The elevator rumbled as it moved upward.

"Once we arrive, let's split up and clear the floor as quickly as possible, then reconvene at the elevator. Don't leave anyone alive unless they're in chains," Cain instructed them.

The elevator doors opened with a *bing*. A woman with a neat brown bob and an old rose suit glanced up from her seat behind the reception desk, frowning at them. Her aura outed her as a vampire.

"I got her." Drawing her saber, Sarah sprinted toward the woman while Lilah and Cain took the left and right hallway, respectively.

"Security!" the woman shouted.

"Damn." With one swing of her saber, Sarah decapitated her. "Too late."

Based on the sounds of movement from behind a

door next to the reception, the woman's shouting had not gone unnoticed.

"Keep going. I'll stay and take care of anyone who heard her screaming," he said.

She nodded and followed the hallway up ahead.

He tightened the grip on his sword as the door opened and two tall vampires emerged, wearing a black uniform with the word "SECURITY" printed in white. One of them had a head of curly blond hair, the other one was black-haired with a low fade cut. Both gaped at the headless corpse on the chair behind the desk and then at him.

"Another Van Helsing wannabe? You'll regret this," the black-haired vampire said. Metallic knuckles gleamed on his fingers.

"Let's see how you like losing your head." The blond one drew a sword.

He gulped but did not back down. Hopefully, they'd underestimate him.

When the black-haired one attacked with the knuckles, he braced and took a hit to the guts. The punch knocked the air out of him, but instead of doubling over, he gritted his teeth and pierced the vampire's heart with a calculated thrust. The body fell to the floor with a *thump*.

"What the hell?" The other vampire lunged at him.

Dave staggered back a few feet—the previous attack had taken a toll—and raised his weapon with both hands on the handle to fend the vampire off. Their swords clashed, and the force of their collision vibrated through his body.

Ceaselessly, the vampire battered his sword, pushing him back until he reached the wall.

"Damn." He groaned.

The vampire swung his sword for a final blow, which never came. Cain tackled him from the side. After wrestling him to the ground, he plunged a dagger through his heart, killing him instantly. Not for the first time, Dave appreciated having Cain as an ally instead of a foe.

"Good timing…Thanks," he said.

"You're welcome." Cain rummaged through the corpse's pockets.

"Any luck finding an ID card on him?"

"No. How about the other one?"

He checked the pockets of the black-haired vampire, but they were empty except for a lanyard with a chip. "Maybe this is it?"

"Possibly. The other guy got one around his neck as well."

They took the lanyards and then waited by the elevator.

Sarah joined them a couple of minutes later. "Are you all right?"

Dave nodded. "A bit shaken from the fight. You?"

"I only faced a handful of clerks. Most didn't know what hit them."

Lilah appeared in front of the elevator, pouting. "Same here. They were not even worth the effort."

"Yeah," Cain agreed. "Looks like Dave was the only one facing a real challenge."

He sighed. "Lucky me."

Chapter 30

When the elevator doors opened to the twelfth floor, a vaguely familiar energy sent icy tingles down Sarah's spine. Who did this aura belong to? Either way, their death was inevitable. She balled her fists and braced herself to confront her past again. "There's someone I aspire to kill here. Please take care of the other vampires. And don't get in my way."

Without awaiting a reply, she headed toward the ominous aura.

She strode past several offices filled with vampires working late. Although the sound of their fingers tapping on keyboards and murmured conversations reached her ears, she didn't even spare them a glance.

When she opened the door to the corner office at the end of the hallway, the rich aroma of jasmine filled her senses. A stern, slim-faced woman in a gray skirt suit, wearing glasses, stared at her from a desk with a laptop and neatly stacked papers. As if a vampire required glasses. For her, they served as some sort of weird fashion statement.

"Sarah."

"Mathilda."

The woman pushed the glasses up her nose, and the gesture triggered a short flashback.

They'd been training outside for hours without sleep or food. Rain pattered down onto the muddy ground, making it slick and wet. All the while, Mathilda watched them from the doorway with a scratch pad and a stopwatch, jotting down notes. Everyone knew the numbers on her list determined who would get dinner. And the time of judgment neared. She pushed up her glasses. "Sarah, sweety, your average was two seconds slower than last week. Maybe a night of fasting will improve your score."

Well, tonight, Mathilda wouldn't get *her* dinner. Not tonight, nor ever again.

"So, you caused the commotion downstairs." Mathilda sighed. "Give me a second."

Too perplexed to react, she only frowned while Mathilda picked up her smartphone and dialed a number. It rang twice before someone answered.

"Change of plans," Mathilda said. "Do it now."

After disconnecting the call, she crushed the phone in her hand and smirked.

A wave of unease surged through Sarah. "What plans?"

"You'll find out soon enough. I know you'll kill me. Even if I can't change my fate, I can ensure you'll lose in the long run." Mathilda leaned back in her chair, folding her hands. "Go on then, dig your grave."

She tightened the grip on her saber. Was killing her a mistake?

"Don't let her toy with your mind." Dave appeared behind her, placing an encouraging hand on her shoulder.

She inhaled deeply, feeling her chest rise. "You're right. She's already controlled my life for too long."

Mathilda didn't even attempt to run when she came for her head and cut it off with a clean strike. Even as it tumbled to the floor, the unnerving smirk never left her lips.

The hair on the back of her neck lifted at the sight. "What if she wasn't bluffing?"

"Then we'll deal with it. Together." He flashed her a reassuring smile and offered her his hand to lead her back to the elevator, where Lilah and Cain waited.

Lilah practically glowed with excitement. "We've exterminated the remaining vampires on this floor. Based on the energy I feel, they've assembled their strongest fighters upstairs."

"Aren't you worried?" she asked.

"Not with Cain by my side," Lilah answered.

She looked at Dave, and her heart constricted. Having him by her side felt good, but it scared her at the same time. She vowed not to let any of the beasts upstairs take him from her. "Let's go."

Once they entered the elevator, Cain used the chip on the lanyard to send them to the top floor.

The upper level comprised an enormous hall with a black onyx marble floor. The morning sun bathed everything in light, yet the rays didn't even tickle her skin. Large, coated windows blocked the UV radiation.

Three silver thrones stood in the center of the room. A woman in a white dress with pinned-up, golden-blonde hair throned on the biggest one in the middle, whereas two men occupied the ones to her left and right.

When they stepped out of the elevator, over a dozen armed vampires encircled them.

"Are you the runaway soldier all the fuss was about?" The woman on the throne asked in a plummy voice, narrowing her eyes on her. "You're so young…You could've had a future with us."

She mustered Lilah and Cain next and scoffed. "And

you? I'd recognize the obnoxious vibe in your aura anywhere. He sent you, didn't he? That insufferable fool of an ex-husband. I asked him for help, not for even more assassins out for my head."

"Wait, what?" Lilah asked.

"Huh. He didn't even mention me to you? How amusing." The queen's loud laughter echoed through the room. "Then let me fill you in. I was married to your fool of a king from the moment of his coronation, more than a millennium ago, until I tired of my role as his wife. He didn't grant me the respect I deserved, so I left and founded my own kingdom."

"You're doing such a poor job as queen..." Lilah said. "Maybe you should have stayed and learned from him instead."

"Outrageous. Kill them!" the queen bellowed.

All hell broke loose as the horde of vampires attacked.

Sarah slashed, thrust, and kicked at anything moving in her vicinity. With every limb she severed and every heart she pierced, blood soiled her clothes, the floor, and everything around her. Soon, it colored her vision red. Yet the wave of enemies didn't subside, and she kept fighting. Like a machine, she moved without pondering her actions. Time lost all meaning as she cut through her enemies. The adrenaline rushing through her body fueled her inner beast, and it frolicked in the carnage.

She only registered the cuts and bruises on her body once everything quieted down. Her heart sank in her chest when she took in her surroundings. Body parts covered the floor. Lilah and Cain stood back-to-back a few meters from her, panting, their clothes drenched in their enemies' blood. But where was Dave?

A groan drew her to a pile of corpses. She pushed the remnants of an oversized bald-headed man aside to reveal Dave. "Are you okay?"

His face contorted. "Not really."

She freed him from the remnants of their enemies. Bite marks and scratches covered most of his body, and his right arm was bent in an unnatural way. At least he was still breathing.

"Drink my blood." After biting into her wrist, she offered it to him. He gladly accepted.

A dramatic sigh from behind shifted her attention to the queen on her throne. The royal family remained.

"If you want something done right, better do it yourself." The queen put on a pair of gloves and rose to her feet. "Come on, boys."

One of the princes—a fresh-faced, pretty boy with short, blond hair—followed her at once. His aura put him at around a century.

The other one felt much older. Yet the tall, black-haired prince leaned back in his throne, scratching his chin as he watched them.

"Markus, will you not stand with me against our enemies?" the queen asked him.

"I will not."

"Unbelievable. You'll pay for your pig-headedness after I'm done with them." The queen fetched a whip from her handbag, cracking its tip with a swift flick of her wrist.

The blond prince drew a rapier. "We don't need him to exterminate these vermin."

"Sarah, can you handle the prince?" Lilah asked. "Cain and I will face the queen."

A glance at Dave revealed he was not up for another

fight yet. Could she protect him and defeat the prince? Only one way to find out. "Sure."

Chapter 31

Once again, Dave watched helplessly while Sarah fought for their lives. He balled his fists, and the action sent a searing pain through his shoulder. Would he ever be able to fight by her side without holding her back?

She dueled with the blond prince, and the blades of their weapons chinked every time they clashed against each other. Her movements were slower than usual. Even if most of the blood on her clothes stemmed from her enemies, she'd suffered deep wounds as well. Like him, she needed a break. How much more could she take?

Meanwhile, Lilah and Cain battled the queen. Together, they covered each other's weaknesses and enhanced each other's strengths. With their combined moves, they didn't leave her much room to fight back. Could he support Sarah the same way?

With his remaining power, he forced himself upright. He picked up a sword from the floor, clutched it with his left hand—his right arm hurt too much—and staggered toward her and the prince.

"Stay back," she grunted.

An ugly smile appeared on the prince's face when he spotted him. Then he vanished from where he stood.

Arms like steel grabbed Dave from behind, and an icy hand wrapped around his throat, choking him.

"Surrender, unless you want me to crash his windpipe," the prince said.

"Fuck," he rasped. In addition to being useless, he was an easy target, putting her at risk. Again.

She let go of her saber, and it clattered to the floor. "Don't hurt him."

The fear in her voice cut through his heart like a knife through butter.

The prince laughed until his laughter died in his throat. He jerked and then gasped for air.

Sarah's eyes widened, and Dave turned in the prince's slackening grip to see Markus—the other prince—twisting a dagger in his brother's chest before pulling it out.

"No!" the queen cried out.

The momentary diversion allowed Cain to decapitate her with one forceful strike. Her body sagged down seconds after her son's.

Markus took a step back from Dave, dropped the dagger, and raised his hands. "I'm not your enemy. Please, listen to what I've got to say. But first, don't let her power go to waste. More than a thousand years—drink them up before they seep into nothingness."

Lilah and Cain looked at each other before they both kneeled and bent their heads to drink the blood oozing from the corpse.

Sarah wrinkled her nose in disgust.

Had they won the battle? Somehow, this felt too easy. And yet, his legs gave in from exhaustion.

She caught him before he fell. "Let's sit down."

He nodded, and she helped him to the thrones. He slumped into the biggest one, and she huddled against him.

"I'm glad you're alive," she whispered.

He tilted her head up and pressed a kiss to her lips.

When her dreamy eyes met his, he nearly lost himself in them.

Markus cleared his throat, drawing his attention away from her.

As the flow of blood from the queen's body had slackened, Lilah and Cain both picked up their weapons and turned toward Markus.

"So, speak," Cain said.

Markus took another step back and bowed to them. "I am Markus, child of your king, born to darkness in 1561. My *mother*—although not by blood—took me with her when she claimed the New World. I never saw eye-to-eye with her extreme views. And yet I lacked the allies to stand against her. Biding my time, I waited for those destined to bring her demise—you."

"So, we did. What is it you aspire to do now?" Cain asked.

"Someone will have to fill the power vacuum you created. Do you fancy someone willing to repent and bow to your king—my father—ruling the States, or do you prefer to leave the seat open for a possible new threat?" Markus' eyes fell on Sarah. "Unless *you* want to govern over them all. But I have an inkling your talent lies more in hunting those who've overstepped than in ruling our people. And I applaud your cause.

"We should not be so bold as to step into the light, kill for fun, or force children into a life of servitude. My words fell on deaf ears until now. Please believe me when I say I had no part in your torture, and I am deeply sorry." He looked back at Cain. "I ask you to give me the chance to right my mother's wrongs."

"Since we're only here to support her, your fate lies in her hands." Cain turned to Sarah.

She took a deep breath and studied Markus intently. "A fortnight ago, I'd have insisted on your death because I viewed all vampires as evil. Now, I'm willing to give you the benefit of the doubt. After all, I can't kill every vampire. And not every one of us deserves death."

Dave's lips parted slightly in wonder, and a heavy weight lifted off his chest. Had she finally stopped equating vampires with pure evil?

"I am pleased about your change of heart." Cain smiled at her before facing Markus. "I'm still interested in the king's judgment on this matter. Would you accompany me? If you speak the truth, he'll surely welcome you back to the family."

"Of course," Markus said.

After asking Lilah to stay and keep an eye out for any vampires showing up to challenge Sarah and him in their current condition, Cain teleported away with Markus.

"How about I check the building for any human captives and release them while you two take some time to recover?" Lilah suggested.

"Sounds good, thanks," he said.

Once Lilah disappeared, Sarah huddled even closer to him. "We did it…Without their royal family, some vampires responsible for my kidnapping may still be out there, but they pose less of a threat."

"We've still got plenty of time to find them," he said. "For now, let's return home and figure out how this relationship thing can work between us."

"I like that idea." She smiled.

Something vibrated in his pants pocket. When he pulled out his phone, Emily was calling. With a frown, he answered. "Hello?"

"Dave?" Emily sounded breathless. "A small group of vampires attacked the compound."

"What?" His heart skipped a beat. "Is everyone all right?"

Silence. Then, "No. Lily and the other kids...they've been kidnapped."

A wave of dizziness washed over him, and all warmth drained from his body. Sarah tensed in his arms.

"There is more. The vampires left a message. Let me read it to you—" Something rustled at the other end of the phone. " 'Tell your little vampire whore to surrender to us. If she does not, your children will suffer an excruciating death. She's got until dusk to come to the place where we created her, alone and unarmed.' "

Without a word, Sarah got up and paced in front of the thrones.

"Don't even think about listening to their demands," he said to her. Then he told Emily, "We'll save them, don't worry."

With shaking hands, he ended the call. After staring at the screen for a moment, he put it away. When he looked up again, Sarah was gone.

"Damn it." His head was spinning, and his heart thudded dully in his chest.

Of course, she'd sacrifice herself in a heartbeat. And why had Cain insisted on teaching her how to teleport, making it all too easy for her to rush to her ruin?

But he would not lose her. Not like this.

Chapter 32

According to Cain, the secret to a successful teleportation lay in visualizing all the details of her destination, including smells and emotions she associated with it. Well, Sarah felt more than strongly about this desolate and remote farm. Her skin crawled at the thought of ever setting foot in the building again. And just remembering the moldy scent of her former bedroom made her nauseous. Yet here she was. She would not let Lily, Tim, and Anthony suffer in her stead. Better her than them.

The tiny room she'd grown up in hadn't changed. The bare chamber's yellowed walls encompassed two thin mattresses, both with a thin wool blanket and a flattened pillow, next to a cardboard box filled with run-down clothes. A blood-stained sweater on top reminded her of the night they'd turned her, sending a chill down her spine. Without electricity in the house, light only reached the inside through a small window.

The floorboard creaked as she stepped out of the room and into the hallway. "I'm here now. Alone and unarmed. Let the kids go."

"We said nothing about letting them go," a cold, familiar voice sounded from the basement.

"I'm not here to play games, Dylan. Release them."

"We never play games." Dylan pushed the creaky basement door open and stepped into the foyer. With his slicked-back, greasy, black hair and a mustache, the vampire still had the same sleazy air she'd despised about him for years. "You seem to think you can make demands. You can't. Let me tell you how this will go. You surrender yourself completely to us, and we'll let the kids *grow up*. While you waste away in our dungeon—a secret weapon to use whenever we please— we'll turn them into our newest soldiers."

"No!" She took a threatening step toward him.

He raised his finger in warning. "Don't. Think carefully before you act, or your beloved kids will suffer for your deeds. Pascal is with them right now, ready to skin them alive on my command."

She froze on the spot, clenching her teeth so hard her jaw hurt. Pascal—her sire—loved inflicting pain on others. He was a short guy with an unhealthy interest in knives and daggers.

"Why are you doing this?" she asked in a carefully controlled tone.

"To create an unstoppable army."

"What for? Your queen is dead."

"Really?" An ugly smile appeared on his face. "Well, we suspected as much after Mathilda's call. Even better. That leaves all the power for us to grab. No one will dare stand in our way."

She swallowed hard. How could she get out of this situation without endangering the kids? Giving up her freedom for theirs was one thing, but standing idly by while these monsters forced them into slavery? And it was all her fault. Without her selfish desire to live among humans, the vampires would've never targeted them.

Somehow, she had to save them, even if it cost her life.

****

Dave paced in front of the thrones, his heart raging in his chest. "Why aren't they back yet?"

"Relax." Lilah sighed. "With the time difference, the king might not have risen yet. And reuniting with his long-lost son after centuries takes longer than a couple of minutes. Why don't you rest? Your human body needs a break sometimes."

"As if I could rest. Give me some blood and I'll be fine."

She rolled her eyes. "It's not a cure for everything. Besides, if we run after her with no plan and no backup, the situation will only worsen. And we've got no clue where they are."

"I know." Groaning, he forcefully kicked against the nearest throne. He cried out as pain shot through his big toe. How was he supposed to keep a clear head and make a plan with Sarah in peril? And the kids…what if they didn't make it? His breathing quickened, yet there was not enough air in his lungs. His chest felt unusually tight. What if he couldn't save them?

Lilah appeared in front of him. Grabbing both his arms, she pushed him against the wall. He struggled against her grip, but when her eyes bored into his, everything around them vanished. "You. Need. To. Rest. Now."

Her words echoed in his mind, and his eyelids became heavy. After a short prick on his neck—had she bitten him?—instant sleep overcame him.

The voices of Markus and Cain woke him. He blinked his eyes open and looked around. He lay on the ground with a blanket wrapped around his body. Stars were gleaming outside. How long had he slept?

"Good, you're awake," Lilah said.

Heat flushed through his body. "How dare you make me fall asleep?"

She shrugged. "You were already hyperventilating. So, you needed a break."

"That doesn't give you the right to control my mind!"

"Don't we have more pressing matters to address?" Markus said. "Lilah has updated us on the situation. I know the perpetrators and some of the places where they usually reside. We can check them one by one."

"I might have a better idea. Give me a second." With luck, Sarah was still wearing her neck ring. And if she was still wearing it, then…His hands shook as he fetched his phone and opened the tracking app Ian had installed. He hadn't thought he'd ever resort to it, but now he was glad for the hidden GPS tracker. After loading for two minutes, a red dot appeared around fifty miles west.

"Do you know this place?" he asked Markus.

Markus nodded. "Yes, and I can take you there."

****

Dylan locked Sarah into a cell—or rather, a broom closet with reinforced, silver-coated walls and no window.

She slouched onto the ground. Sturdy, thick, silver manacles bound her wrists and ankles. Tiny spikes adorned the shackles, piercing her skin. They drained her energy, and thus kept her weak and unable to teleport away. She had no intention of running and leaving the kids, anyway.

Their hearts galloped in the adjoining room, and the air reeked of their fear. But as long as they were afraid, they lived. She wished she could comfort them with a fairy tale or something to take their minds off this gruesome place.

Unfortunately, the kids were right to be scared. Apart from Pascal and Dylan, she felt two more vampires in the house—two very young and powerful ones. Based on the crazed hunger tainting their auras, they were less than a week old, which made them extremely dangerous for any human in their vicinity.

Chapter 33

Markus teleported them to a fallow field in front of an old farmhouse in the middle of nowhere. By the looks of it, the decaying building stemmed from the beginning of the previous century, and its owners had never bothered to renovate. White paint was flaking off the wall, and most of the green wooden window shutters were askew, while others were missing entirely. Had Sarah truly grown up in such a bleak place?

"I detect the auras of five vampires inside," Cain said. "Sarah is among them."

Dave tightened his fists. "Let's storm the house before they notice us."

"Too late," Lilah said.

Three vampires exited the house—a blond man followed by two girls who couldn't be older than sixteen or seventeen. And yet, the man was a head shorter than them.

When Markus stepped forward, the man bowed to him. "To what do we owe the pleasure of your visit, Markus?"

"This is not a social call, Pascal," Markus said. "It's come to my attention you kidnapped several kids to force another vampire to do your bidding. I can't allow such behavior."

Pascal crossed his arms and jutted his chest out. "Good thing you've got no say in the matter, then. I've heard about the queen's demise, and I don't recognize you as her successor. Now, unless you wish to play with my newest offspring, I suggest you leave."

"We're not going anywhere," Dave said.

"Oh look, the food is talking." Pascal's eyes narrowed on him. "Girls, take care of these intruders. You may feast on the human."

A guttural sound escaped one girl. Her dark, almond-shaped eyes glowed overly bright as they fixated on him. "Perfect, I'm starving."

"Leave something for me, Selena." The other one growled and jumped at Dave, who drew his sword to fend her off.

"Don't start without me." Selena threw herself at him as well.

Lilah intercepted her with her staff. "I'll help Dave with this one. Cain, Markus, follow Pascal and secure the house."

"You sure you can take one, Dave?" Cain asked. "They're young and rabid."

While the girls occupied him, Pascal had made his way back inside. If he hurt Sarah or the kids, Dave could never forgive himself. "I'll be fine. Save them!"

With a nod, Cain and Markus hurried after Pascal.

He studied his opponent. With her short, blonde hair, blue eyes, and slim figure, she reminded him of an even younger Sarah. Had she suffered a similar fate? "What's your name?" he asked.

She stared blankly ahead, as if she didn't hear his question.

He tried again. "You don't have to fight. There are other options for you, you know?"

With an animalistic roar, she charged at him again,

pounding on him, his sword, and anything within her reach.

"You won't get through to her. She's crazed with hunger," Lilah yelled in between exchanging blows with Selena.

He tightened his grip on the weapon. Could he kill someone so young? The poor girl had never had a chance at life. Just like Sarah.

He swung his sword at her, and she blocked it with her left arm. His blade cut through her skin and bone, severing her hand. The girl screamed as blood gushed from her wrist.

She hurled herself at him, throwing him down and pinning him to the ground with surprising force. He rammed his sword into her side, and it cut through her torso. Yet the injury didn't deter her. Without even flinching, she snapped at him. He pushed against her, but she overpowered him and gouged her fangs into his throat.

The agonizing pain and whatever she injected him with paralyzed him. Helplessly, he lay on the ground as she ripped into his throat. He opened his mouth to scream, but only a gurgling sound escaped him. Blood left his body at a frightening speed, and he grew colder with every ounce. Had she torn out his jugular?

A sickening iciness overtook him, and everything around him faded slowly into nothingness. Was this the end? How would Sarah deal without him? He'd do anything to see, hold, and kiss her one last time.

"Fuck, Dave!" Lilah's panicked voice was the last thing he heard.

****

Sighing, Sarah clutched her arms around her legs.

They were fighting for her and the kids while she cowered helplessly in the dark. Not only Lilah and Cain had come to their rescue—she recognized Markus' aura as well. The distinctive vibes of their royal blood made them easily recognizable. Was Dave with them? If she hadn't acted rashly, she could've fought next to him. Instead, she was a useless captive, unable to save herself or the ones she cared about.

Grinding her teeth, she pulled on the chains again, but they were too sturdy. The action pushed the silver spikes deeper into her skin, bringing tears to her eyes. Despite her inhuman abilities, she was too weak to make a difference. Her vision blurred as tears flooded her eyes, and she curled into a ball on the ground.

After what felt like an eternity, a loud crash ripped her from her melancholy. She wiped her eyes and looked up in time to see Cain breaking the door to her prison with a forceful kick.

His eyebrows drew together. "Are you okay?"

She was a pathetic pile of flesh and bones with puffy eyes, so not really. Still, she nodded.

"Let me get those chains off you." Wrapping his hands in cloth from his coat to prevent the silver from affecting him, he broke the manacles with brute force.

"Thanks." She stood up.

"I think your kids are in the room next door. Do you want to get them yourself, or are you too hungry?"

As if she'd ever hurt them. "I can handle the hunger."

"Good. I'll help the others with the remaining vampires. Let's meet up outside." Cain vanished down the hall.

She inspected the door to the kids' room. With a

pointed kick to the handle, she broke it.

A gasp sounded from within, and the door swung open to reveal Lily, Tim, and Anthony huddling together in the far corner.

When she stepped inside, they looked at her with gigantic eyes.

"Sarah?" Tim asked.

"Hey. I've come to your rescue." She smiled at them.

The kids leaped to their feet, ran up to her, and encircled her in a hug.

"Thank God you're here." Lily sobbed.

Their warmth and vitality sent a shudder through her body, and her mouth watered at their sweet aroma. Maybe being close to the kids without having fed was not one of her brightest ideas.

She clenched her jaw and wiggled out of their hug. "Let's get you outside."

Taking Lily and Anthony by the hand, she led the three kids out of the house. From the corner of her eye, she glimpsed the corpse of her sire in one of the rooms they passed. The sight didn't grant her any satisfaction. Funny how little her revenge mattered in the grand picture.

She froze when she exited the front door.

Markus, Cain, and Lilah were standing in a semicircle around three bodies on the ground. One of them looked awfully familiar.

"No," she whispered. Letting go of the kids' hands, she sprinted forward.

A wave of nausea rolled over her, accompanied by a ringing in her ears. "It can't be."

With shaking limbs, she fell to her knees next to his

body. "Dave!"

She was vaguely aware of the kids arriving at her side, calling his name, and asking if he'd be all right. Yet she could not answer them.

An agonizing scream tore from her throat. He'd died because of her. Her stupid quest for revenge and her impulsiveness. Her chest tightened, and a stabbing pain pervaded her heart.

When Lilah put a hand to her shoulder, she lunged at her.

Cain and Markus grabbed her, holding her back.

"Sarah, please calm down and listen to me for a moment," Lilah said in a controlled voice.

"Calm down? Why?" She sobbed. "He's dead!"

"Yes, for now. But there's a chance to bring him back."

Chills seeped through her body. "What are you saying?"

"When I got to him, it was too late to save his life. But I injected him with the fluid to keep his soul locked in his body. As you know, it's the first step toward turning a human."

Chapter 34

"I won't turn him into a monster." Sarah balled her shaking hands into fists. "For God's sake, he's a vampire hunter!"

"Yet you—a vampire—have fought by his side all this time," Lilah said. "To him, you're no monster."

"Accepting me and wanting to become like me are two different things."

Lilah shrugged. "Based on the fragments of his thoughts I caught over the last few days, he sometimes hated his humanity because it restricted his abilities. So, I believe he'd be open to the idea. Unfortunately, we can't ask him, so the decision falls to you."

"And we won't turn him," Cain added. "It's your choice and your responsibility. If you decide against it, we can still burn his body and thus grant him true death."

"So, you expect me to choose between letting the man I love die for good and forcing him to live as a beast?" She snarled at him.

"I understand your struggle." His gaze softened. "I faced the same impossible choice once, although the circumstances differed. Turning Lilah went against everything I believed in, yet I could not imagine life without her."

"Appreciate the chance you've got here," Markus said. "Eternity is longer than you might realize. If you find someone to share your life with, don't let him slip away."

But how could she decide his fate based on her selfish desires?

Someone pulled at her dress. When she turned toward the source, she faced the kids, watching her with tears in their eyes.

"I'm not really sure I understand what's going on. Can you bring him back?" Lily asked.

She nibbled on her lip. "Theoretically, yes. But only as a vampire."

"Sounds good, as long as he's like you." Anthony smiled sheepishly at her.

She struggled to find the words to explain her hesitation to them. "He won't be the same as before."

"That's okay, as long as we don't lose him." Lily swallowed hard.

"Please bring him back to us." Fresh tears streamed down Tim's face.

Their innocent pleas melted her heart. How could she deny their wish if she secretly longed for the same thing?

She drew a deep breath and turned to Cain. "What do I need to do?"

"Feed him your blood. As several minutes have passed since his death, he'll require a large amount—at least two or three liters. Can you handle losing so much?"

"I'll manage. Get the kids away from here, please."

Lilah stepped forward and opened her arms as if inviting them for a hug. "All right, you three. Come here."

The kids glanced at Sarah. When she nodded encouragingly, they went into Lilah's waiting embrace.

Holding them close, she teleported away.

Cain handed her a dagger. "I recommend cutting your throat for a first big gush of blood. Force it into his mouth."

After taking a few calming breaths, she kneeled by Dave's face and bent forward. She tilted his head back and carefully forced his mouth open. With trembling hands, she put the blade to her jugular and cut deeply.

Unable to scream with the dagger in her throat, her body shook in agony as the silver burned her flesh. Yet she forced the blade even deeper to maintain a steady blood flow.

The seconds ticked by, and she became dizzy from the blood loss. Her stomach constricted, demanding a fresh meal. How much more could she give?

What if she failed to bring him back?

Something changed in the air. A stream of energy swirled around them and accumulated in Dave's body. She sagged in relief when his heart thumped once beneath her, and the dagger slipped from her hands.

Cain steadied her before she fell over. "You're close, but he needs even more blood to regain consciousness. You can feed him from your wrist now."

She groaned and sat back as the wound on her throat healed. Using her fangs, she tore into her wrist. When she held it over his mouth, a shudder went through his body.

His canines grew into fangs, and he snapped at her, sinking his teeth into her flesh.

"It's an instinctual reaction to the taste of blood," Cain explained. "He's close now."

Dave's throat began to work and swallowed the blood he was sucking from her veins with a frightening intensity. With every gulp, her body became colder and number. Yet she willed him to keep drinking so he'd rise again.

His body jerked, and his eyes blinked open. His bite loosened, and he released her wrist. "Sarah? What...?"

All the tension left her body, and she collapsed onto him.

****

"What happened?" Dave sat up, maneuvering the limp form of Sarah onto his lap.

Everything felt wrong. Although night colored the sky black, his surroundings seemed brighter than usual and surprisingly sharp. His eyes wandered from the vampires surrounding him to a birch at the edge of the field, and he noticed a cobweb spanning its leaves.

A mix of exotic scents caused his mouth to water, and he licked his lips. Dried blood covered his face, throat, and clothes. Why didn't he taste its usual metallic flavor?

"What do you remember?" Cain asked. His voice sounded deeper than before.

He frowned. "I fought against the young vampire, and she ripped my throat out. Sarah must have given me quite a bit of blood to heal me. I feel weird. Is she okay?"

"She will be." Cain squatted down to his eye level. "Sarah didn't heal you. You died. With our help, she brought you back as a vampire."

He blinked at him several times. "What?"

Cain's words explained his weird perception. But the Sarah he knew would not create another vampire. She despised her kind too much. Had she put aside her prejudice for him?

"You're one of us now," Markus said. "Can you deal

with that?"

He pulled Sarah closer as she stirred. "I don't care what I am. I can deal with anything as long as she's with me."

"Good. Now, we need to get her fresh blood. And it can't hurt if you learn to feed as well," Cain said.

"Then that's my cue to leave," Markus said. "You can handle the rest without me. If you need anything, I'll be at the royal headquarters. Good luck."

"Thank you for your help," Dave said.

Markus nodded and teleported away.

"Okay." He pushed to his feet with Sarah in his arms, carrying her weight with no effort. "Let's go."

Cain put a hand on his shoulder and teleported them to a suburban neighborhood with dozens of detached family homes on well-kept lawns. "Follow my lead."

They headed to the front door of a more secluded house and rang the bell.

A middle-aged man with a beer bottle in his hand opened the door. He gaped at the limp body in Dave's arms and the blood soiling their clothes.

"We had an accident," Cain explained. "Can we use your phone to call nine-one-one?"

"Of course. Come in. Put her on the couch."

The man stepped aside to let them into his home.

While Dave carried Sarah into the living room to lay her down, Cain assaulted the man, sinking his fangs into his flesh. The man gasped, but he had no time to scream before his eyes fell shut and he slipped into a deep slumber. His beer bottle shattered on the floor.

Cain carried him to the couch, cut into his wrist, and held it over Sarah's mouth. "Make sure she drinks. I'll take care of his wife."

"His wife?"

Another heartbeat hammered near the stairs. A woman in a nightgown stared at them with a phone in her hand.

After ripping the phone from her and putting her to sleep with another quick bite, Cain placed the woman in an armchair next to the couch.

The sound of swallowing drew his attention back to Sarah. She was sucking on the man's wrist now, pressing it closer to her mouth with her right hand.

Cain appeared next to them. "With the amount of blood she lost, she won't be able to stop. She doesn't even realize where she is or what she's doing. We need to make sure she doesn't take too much. Listen to his heartbeat. When it slows or thrashes irregularly, his life is in danger."

He closed his eyes to concentrate. The rhythm of the man's heart lulled him into a trance, and everything around him faded. What would his blood taste like?

"Dave, focus." Cain's voice drew him back. "I can't watch both of you at once. I'll teach you to feed once Sarah is better."

The thought of her helped him concentrate on reality. He gritted his teeth. "Sorry."

When the man's heart skipped a few beats, Cain ripped his wrist from her mouth. She snapped at them.

"Hold her down," Cain instructed.

With both hands on her shoulders, Dave pushed her into the couch. She growled, thrashing below him as if her ravenous eyes did not recognize him.

"Sarah, it's me," he said. "Calm down."

"Keep talking," Cain said.

"I'm right here with you. I'm fine, you're fine, and

we defeated your tormentors. Everything's all right."

Slowly, reason returned to her eyes, and she blinked at him. "Dave?"

He smiled at her. "Hi."

"Oh God, I…" She shifted beneath him and lowered her gaze. "How are you?"

He lifted her chin, forcing her to meet his eyes. "I'm fine. More than fine. Thank you for bringing me back to life."

She moved her mouth, but no words came out. He bent down to kiss her, and she melted into him. Her sweet fragrance bewitched him, and when she sucked on his tongue, the intense sensation ignited a fire deep in his core.

Cain cleared his throat behind them. "Dave, I suggest you feed now as well before you lose your composure later."

Dave begrudgingly disentangled from her and fixated his gaze on the woman in the armchair. "Okay. What do I do?"

"I've already made her sleepy, so you can just go for her throat. Sink your fangs into her flesh and will her not to feel any pain. And while you drink, pay attention to her heartbeat."

He swallowed and approached his victim. His insides constricted and his whole body tingled in anticipation. Slowly, he lowered his mouth to her throat and bit her.

A wave of euphoria swamped him as the first drop of blood touched his tongue. The flavor reminded him of his favorite brand of coffee, so rich and with a hint of dark chocolate. Every sip invigorated him, warmth infused his body, and he felt more alive than ever.

Whoever said vampires were dead? Nothing compared to this high.

Sarah gripped his shoulder. "Don't lose yourself. Slow down."

He focused on the pressure of her hand and the sound of the woman's heartbeat. Its constant thudding calmed him. After another sip, he released her.

"Perfect," Sarah praised him. "Now heal her with your blood."

He bit into his finger and healed his bite mark with the forming drops of blood.

"Impressive," Cain said. "Now, let's return to the cabin."

Chapter 35

Lily, Tim, and Anthony huddled against Lilah on the couch, sleeping peacefully. A sense of calm washed over Dave as he watched the rhythmic rise and fall of their chests. Wasn't it ironic how, less than two years ago, the kids sleeping in a vampire's arms would have terrified him?

"Welcome back to the land of the living—or undead." Lilah smiled at him.

"Thanks," he said. "I hope the kids didn't cause you any trouble?"

"Oh no, they're adorable. When they told me they liked fairy tales, I told them one from my hometown— the adventure of four animals who set out to become musicians. It calmed them enough to fall asleep."

A slight lump built in his throat as memories of all the times he read them stories popped up in his head. Their paths would separate now. As a vampire, he was no longer welcome at the compound—their home.

Sarah appeared by his side, taking his hand. He smiled at her. Together, they'd shape their own future.

Lily stirred and looked at him with sleepy eyes. After blinking several times, she gaped at him. "Dave, you're back!"

Her shout woke Tim and Anthony. All three kids ran up to him to give him a hug.

He shivered when he noticed their rapid heartbeats

and breathed in their sweet scent of honey and caramel.

"Kids, step away from Dave, please," Lilah said. "He's not used to being around humans yet, so it's not safe."

"Oh." Their shoulders slumped, but they listened to the warning.

"Can you take them home?" he asked. "I doubt the other hunters would welcome me at the compound right now." He wasn't ready to face them in his new form.

"Yeah, I bet they won't." Lilah laughed. "But I refuse to set foot in your secured building. We can bring them to the main gate or something."

"I'd appreciate it." He smiled. "I'll let them know you're bringing the kids and tell them not to bother you. Do you know how to get there?"

"We can teleport to the picnic area where we met up two weeks ago. Then take your car or something," Cain suggested.

"Do you even know how to drive?"

A smile tugged on Cain's lips. "Although I was born in a time before cars existed, I don't live completely shut off from the world, you know?"

With a sigh, he handed Cain his keys. "Drive carefully."

"Please call them now so we can be off. Walking from the picnic area to your car and driving to the compound will take a while. Besides, I'm sure the two of you have a lot to talk about once you're finally alone." Lilah winked at them.

Rolling his eyes, he scrolled through his phone for Emily's number.

She answered immediately. "Dave, are you all right?"

"Yeah, I'm fine. Listen, we found the kids. Two friends of mine will bring them to the compound shortly. They're vampires, but don't fret. They won't cause any trouble."

"Vampire friends? You've got to be kidding. Why don't you bring the kids?"

"I've got some stuff to deal with. Things I can't explain right now. Anyway, I gotta run. Talk to you later."

He quickly disconnected the call. Then he turned to the kids. "Lilah and Cain will take you home now. You probably won't see me for a while, but I'm always there if you need me. You can call me anytime. Also, please do me a favor and don't tell anyone at the compound what happened to me. It's our little secret, okay?"

Sobbing, the kids nodded.

****

With Lilah, Cain, and the kids gone, Sarah was truly alone with Dave for the first time in two weeks. And so much had changed. Her stomach fluttered at the thought.

"How would you like to spend the remainder of your first night as a vampire?" she asked.

"Oh, I've got an idea or two," he answered with a deep chuckle. "How about we continue where Cain so rudely interrupted us earlier?"

A fire blazed in his eyes as he searched hers. When she licked her upper lip, he pulled her close and slanted his mouth over hers.

With a moan, she surrendered to his tongue, exploring her mouth.

He wrapped his strong arms around her body and guided her backward until the back of her legs touched the edge of the couch. With a push from him, they tumbled onto the furry cushions.

"I've waited so long for us to be alone like this," he whispered. "After almost losing my chance at a future with you, I cannot wait any longer. Will you be mine tonight?"

She swallowed hard, and her body tensed. She'd never been with a man this way. What if she did something wrong? What if she could not live up to his expectations?

"Relax, beautiful." He gently put a strand of her hair behind her ear. "Let me lead you through this."

"Okay."

He unbuttoned his shirt and stripped his still bloody clothes off one by one, dropping them to the floor and giving her a perfect view of the various scars gracing his firm body. They were remnants of his countless battles—proof of a life dedicated to protecting others.

Mesmerized, she traced a scar down his abdomen. When she realized his complete nakedness, she pulled her hand back. Heat rose to her face.

"No need to be shy. I'm all yours." He tilted her head up for another kiss.

While she melted into him, his hands caressed her upper body from her arms to her chest and then to her back in slow, circular movements while skillfully removing her dress and bra.

His fiery gaze explored her body. "Gorgeous."

Her heart thundered as he slid down to kiss and lick her nipple. The unknown sensation sent a surge of desire through her. And when he sucked on it, her body jerked beneath him.

With a smile, he switched to her other breast while his hands wandered to her lower body.

She gasped when his thumb massaged her through the thin fabric of her panties.

"I love how you react to me." His hot breath brushed against her sensitive nipples.

His hand slipped inside her panties, intensifying the experience. An incredible heat built in her core from the simple friction.

"Let me taste you." He slid even farther down and removed her panties. Lowering his head, he licked and sucked on her nub.

Her body trembled as wave after wave of pleasure washed over her, pushing her to new, inexplicable heights.

When he came back up, caught her mouth in a kiss, and pushed two fingers into her, the overload of sensations swept her away like a tsunami.

Even when her mind found its way back to reality, her muscles still spasmed. Could she bring him to such unknown heights as well? She remembered Lilah's unsolicited advice. "Let me try something."

Swapping their positions so she was on top, she let her hands wander along his body. Bending her head to his nipples, she sucked on them. Then she pierced them with her fangs—first one side, then the other—injecting him with the pleasure-inducing fluid.

He moaned as the effect of her bites shook him beneath her. Meanwhile, she explored his body further, kissing his scars and reveling in his tremors.

Once the effects faded, he took ahold of her hips, switching their positions again.

"I yearn to feel all of you." He rubbed his length against her core.

When she shivered in anticipation, he pushed into

her. The first prick of pain turned into a bittersweet feeling of completeness and—most of all—rightness.

"I love you."

"And I love you."

He moved in her rhythmically, bringing them both over the edge in a symphony of passion.

Chapter 36

Lying in bed, Dave watched the lovely woman in his arms sleep. Although they'd spent most of the day enjoying each other's bodies, he felt well rested.

After defeating the tormentors from her past, nothing prevented them from setting out on a new journey toward their future. Together.

Her expression seemed more peaceful and content than anything he'd ever seen on her face. He'd do anything to keep her happy.

Once she stirred, he kissed her cute nose.

Her sleepy gaze met his, and she blushed. "Hey."

"Hello, beautiful."

She wrinkled her brows. "Are you okay? Do you crave blood?"

He kissed the wrinkles away. "I'm more than okay, and I'm not hungry yet. You?"

"I'm good." A smile touched her lips, but it quickly vanished. "Where will we go from here? We can't return to the compound now, with you being a vampire."

"We'll build ourselves a new home. And once I've adjusted to my new self, I can talk to my friends to see if some of them are reasonable enough to give me the benefit of the doubt and work together. Even if they aren't and this is goodbye, I have no regrets."

"What about the kids?"

"They've got many other hunters taking care of

them. And unlike most adults, they are open-minded and know we mean them no harm, so I'm sure we'll meet them again."

"How can you be so optimistic?"

"Easy. I've got you." He pulled her closer into his arms.

A knock sounded on the door. After making sure the blanket covered both of them, he said, "Come in."

Lilah entered. "Sorry, I don't mean to intrude. I just wanted to let you know we're heading home."

"Back to Europe?" he asked.

She nodded.

"How are the kids? Did everything go well last night?" Sarah asked.

"Aside from the two dozen armed hunters who greeted us at our arrival, yes." Lilah chuckled. "Cain drove the car to the main gate, and we teleported away before they could make a move."

"I'm sorry." He sighed. Maybe he'd underestimated his former colleagues' hate for vampires. Luckily, he had all the time in the world to convince them not all vampires were the same.

Lilah shrugged. "No one got hurt, so it's fine. Anyway, I wanted to say goodbye. Our next mission already awaits. Since we won't return to North America anytime soon, you are welcome to stay here and call this cabin your home."

"You sure?" he asked.

"Yeah. Also, if you're looking for a new calling, Markus needs all the help he can get to bring order to his kingdom. He'd employ you as enforcers in a heartbeat. You could hunt vampires in his name, obliterating scumbags who kill for fun or fools who draw attention to our kind. Think about it."

"We will. Thank you."

"Good. Now, enjoy yourselves." Lilah waved goodbye and closed the door behind her.

"Seems like we got the house to ourselves again." He grinned. "Shall we take advantage of it?"

When she smiled at him with sparkling eyes and nodded, he captured her mouth in a kiss.

What a perfect way to start the first night of his new life and their eternity together.

A word about the author...

Elli Morgan was born in 1991 in a small town in Germany. Although she only started learning English in sixth grade, she quickly fell in love with the language. To improve her skills, she spent a year working and traveling in Canada and the US.

As a teenager, she devoured countless fan fiction and vampire novels. During that time, she also developed the idea for her first two books. Her debut, The Waxing Moon, won the Reader Views bronze award in the romance category.

Apart from being a writer, she's also a trained mathematician, working as Business Intelligence Developer at an IT company. In her free time, she enjoys hiking, traveling, and all kinds of games.

For more information, please visit her website at: https://ellimorgan.com

Thank you for purchasing
this publication of The Wild Rose Press, Inc.

For questions or more information
contact us at
info@thewildrosepress.com.

The Wild Rose Press, Inc.
www.thewildrosepress.com